MW00903027

THE USBORNE BO

THE EARTH

Lisa Watts and Jenny Tyler

Illustrated by Bob Hersey
and designed by Bob Scott

Geography Adviser:
Iain Bain, Geographical Magazine

Educational Adviser:
Pamela Bowen, Schools' Advisory
Teacher in Geography

First published in 1976 by Usborne Publishing Ltd,
Usborne House, 83-85 Saffron Hill,
London EC1N 8RT, England.

Copyright © 1986, 1976 Usborne Publishing Ltd.

All rights reserved. No part of this publication may be reproduced, stored in a retrieval system or transmitted in any form or by any means, electronic, mechanical, photocopying or otherwise without the prior permission of the publisher.

The name Usborne and the device are Trade Marks of Usborne Publishing Ltd.

Printed in Belgium

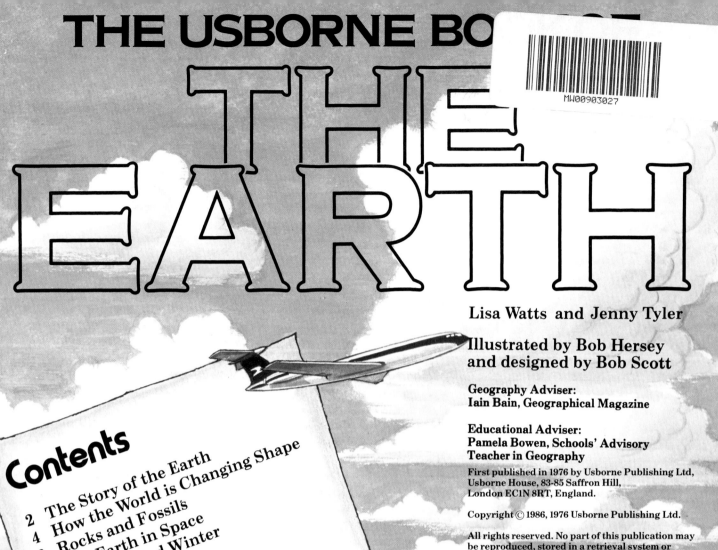

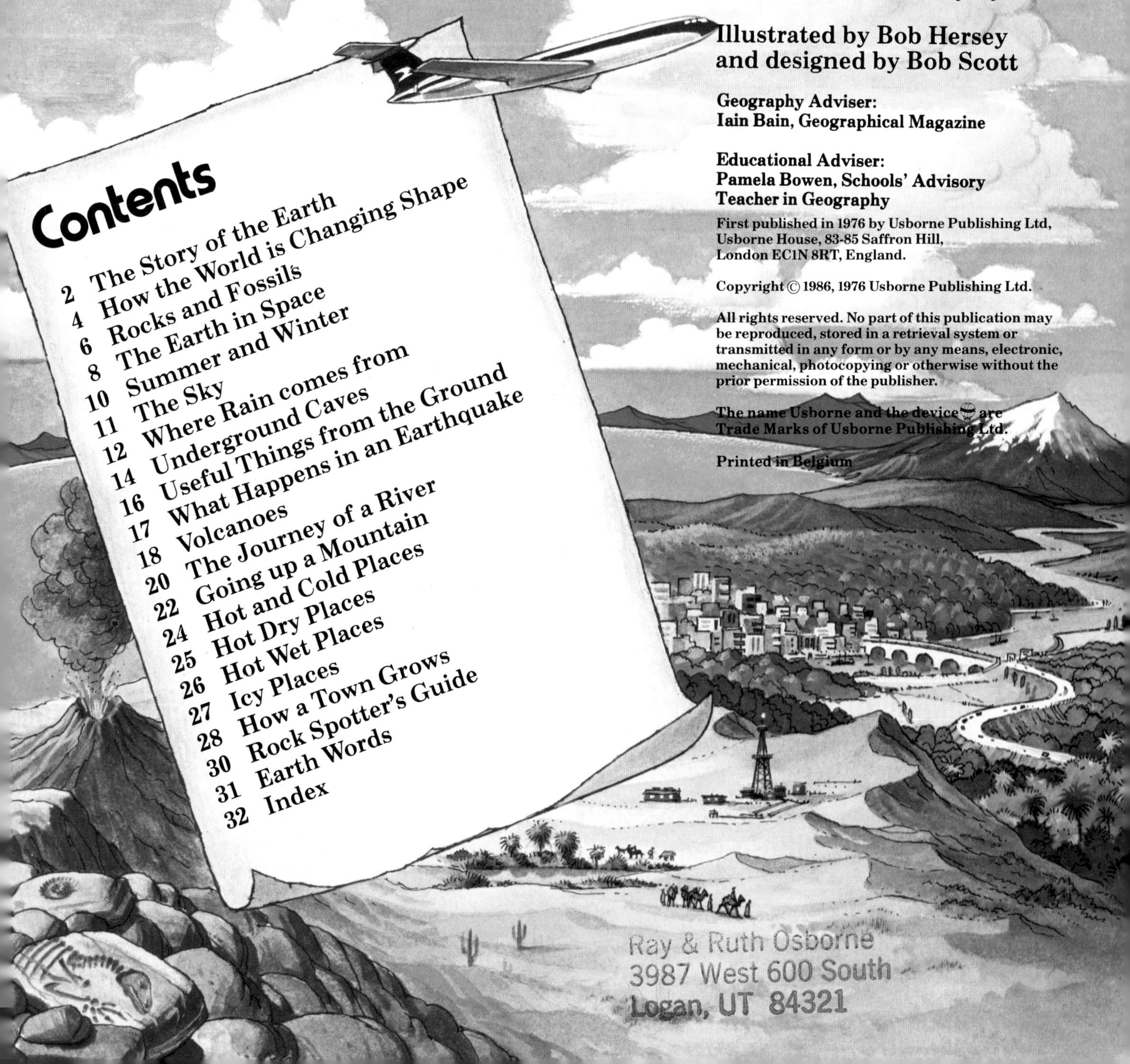

Contents

Ray & Ruth Osborne
3987 West 600 South
Logan, UT 84321

The Story of the Earth

The Earth is about 4,600 million years old. It is hard to imagine such a long time. To help you we have used a huge sand glass.

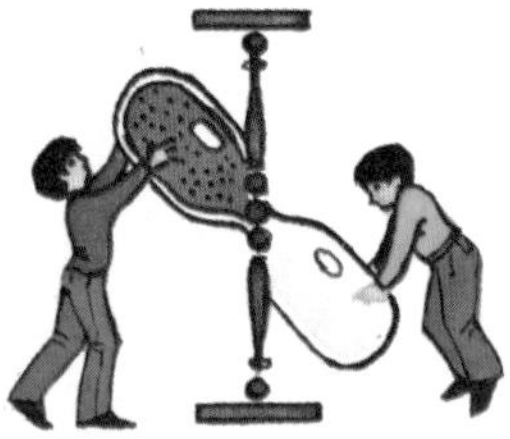

It takes 4,700 million years for the sand to run through it. Watch the sand glass to see how old the Earth is at each stage in the story.

4,700 million years ago

Scientists think the Earth probably began as a great, swirling cloud of dust and gases. This cloud grew very hot and changed into a ball of liquid rock.

4,600 million years ago

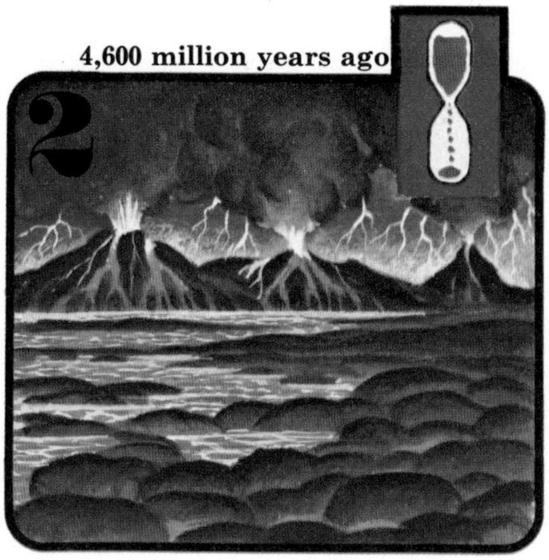

The ball of rock slowly cooled and a thin crust of rock hardened on the outside. Hot, liquid rock from inside broke through the crust in lots of places.

6 **Skeletons give us a good idea of what the first animals looked like. Dinosaurs were a group of animals which lived about 160 million years ago.**

Tree ferns like these still grow in hot, wet places today.
The Stegosaurus had three brains, though none of them were very big. It had one brain in its head, one in its tail and one in its back.
One of the first flying animals was called the Rhamphorhynchus. It was hairy and had sharp teeth in its beak.
The huge Brontosaurus only ate plants. From its nose to its tail it was about 22 metres.

3,800 million years ago

3

Enormous clouds of steam and gases collected round the Earth. There were violent storms and rain poured down from the clouds. Floods made the first seas.

2,500 million years ago

4

Plants began to grow in the seas, though there were no animals yet. Animals cannot live without oxygen gas to breathe and at first there was no oxygen.

570–400 million years ago

5

As plants grow they make oxygen which animals can breathe. The first animals lived in the sea. Then bigger animals developed and they crawled out on to the land.

The Iguanodon walked upright and could run faster than other dinosaurs. It had spikes like daggers on its thumbs.

7

This picture shows some of the first people on Earth. They lived in caves and made tools out of stone.

There have been people on the Earth for the last million years. This seems a very long time, but look at the sand glass. The last grains of sand have nearly fallen through and people have only just appeared in the story. The Earth existed for about 4,599 million years without any people.

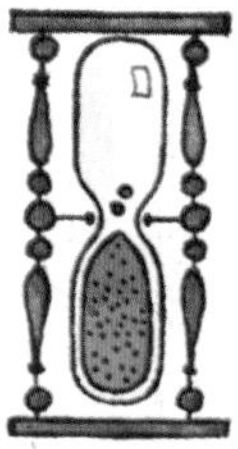

Inside the Earth

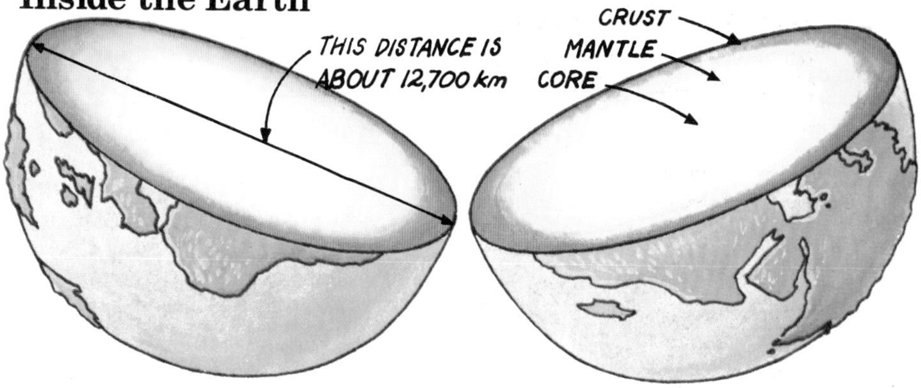
THIS DISTANCE IS ABOUT 12,700 km
CRUST
MANTLE
CORE

If you could cut the Earth in half, it would look something like this.

The *crust* is a thin layer of rock between 8 and 64 kilometres thick.

Beneath the crust, the rock is hot and toffee-like. This part is called the *mantle*. The rock in the mantle is called *magma*.

The centre of the Earth is called the *core*. It is too deep inside the Earth for scientists to examine. But they think it is probably made of very hot, liquid metal.

How the World is Changing Shape

How the land moves

Scientists think that the land is moving very slowly. Find out how this is happening by following the numbers round this picture.

1

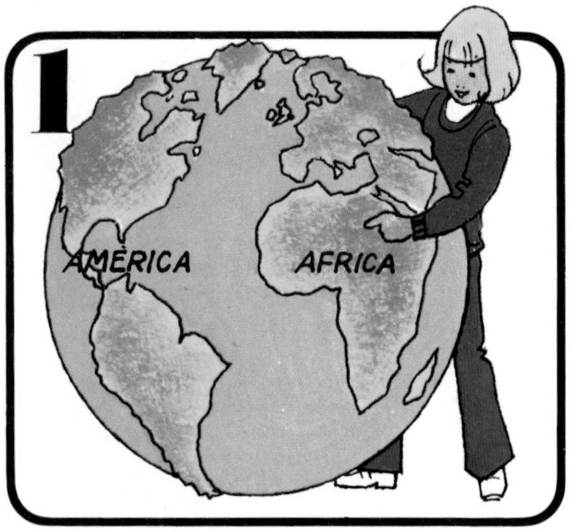

Look at the shapes of Africa and America. The two bits of land look as though they could fit together like jigsaw pieces. Perhaps they were once joined up.

2

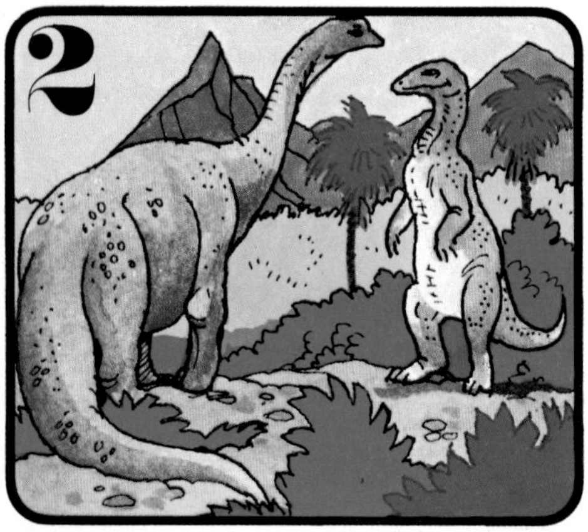

There are dinosaur bones in Africa and in America. The huge animals could not have swum across the sea. But if the land was joined they could have walked across.

3

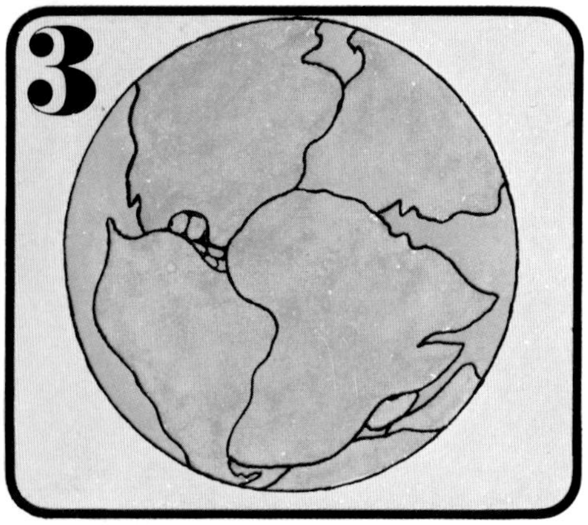

Scientists think the land was once joined up like this. It made one big land called Pangaea. About 190 million years ago, Pangaea began to split up.

4

The land is still moving. Telephone cables under the Atlantic Ocean have snapped because America is moving 25 millimetres away from Europe every year.

5

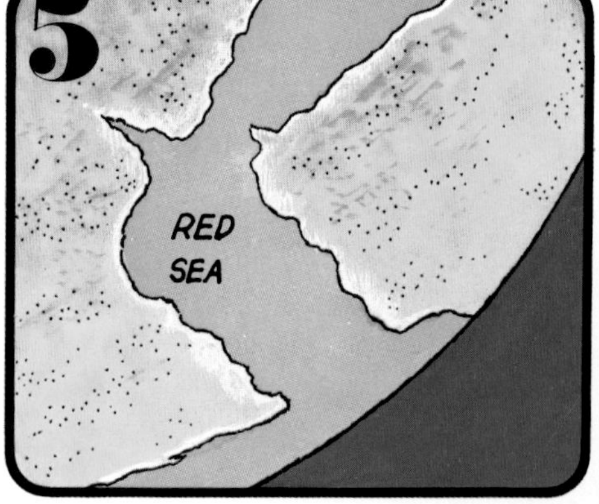

This is what the Red Sea looks like from a space ship. The land seems to have been torn apart. The land is still moving and the Red Sea is getting wider every year.

1 **The Earth's crust is made of pieces which fit very closely together. Each piece is called a *plate*. Here, we have lifted one of the plates up for you to see.**

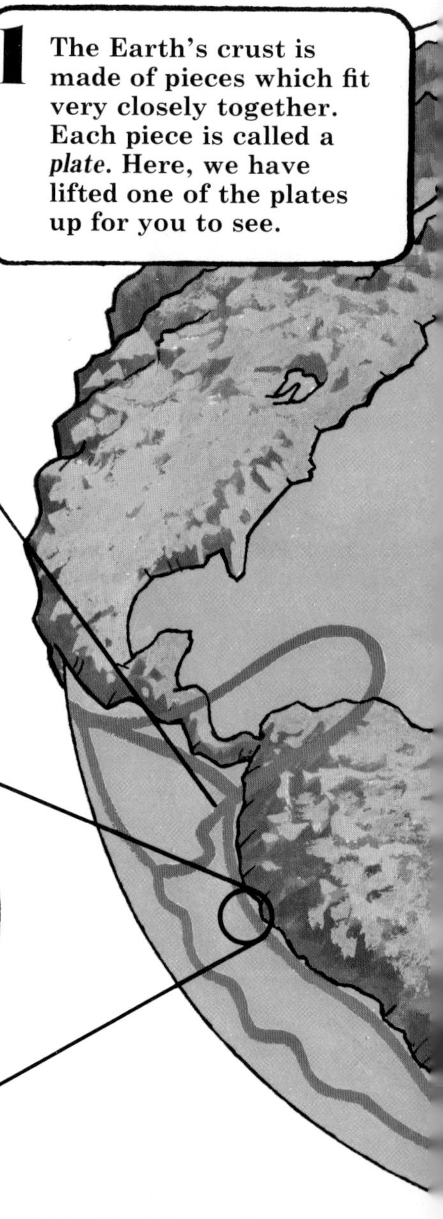

8 **Some plates are moving towards each other. The edge of one plate rides up over the other one. The plate underneath melts as it sinks down into the mantle.**

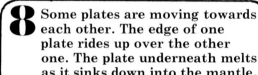

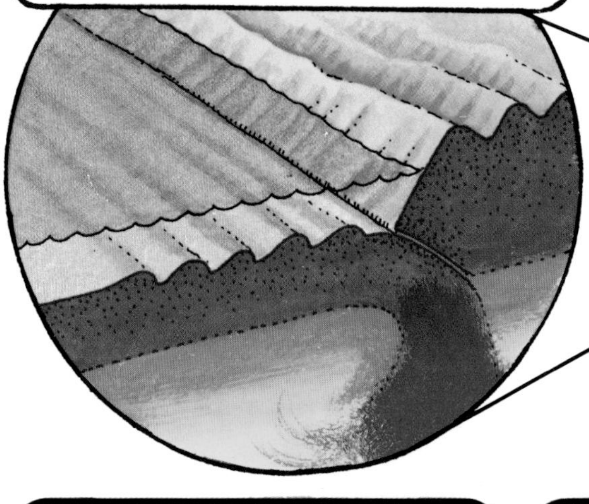

9 **Most of the world's volcanoes and earthquakes happen at the edge of plates because they are weak spots in the Earth's crust.**

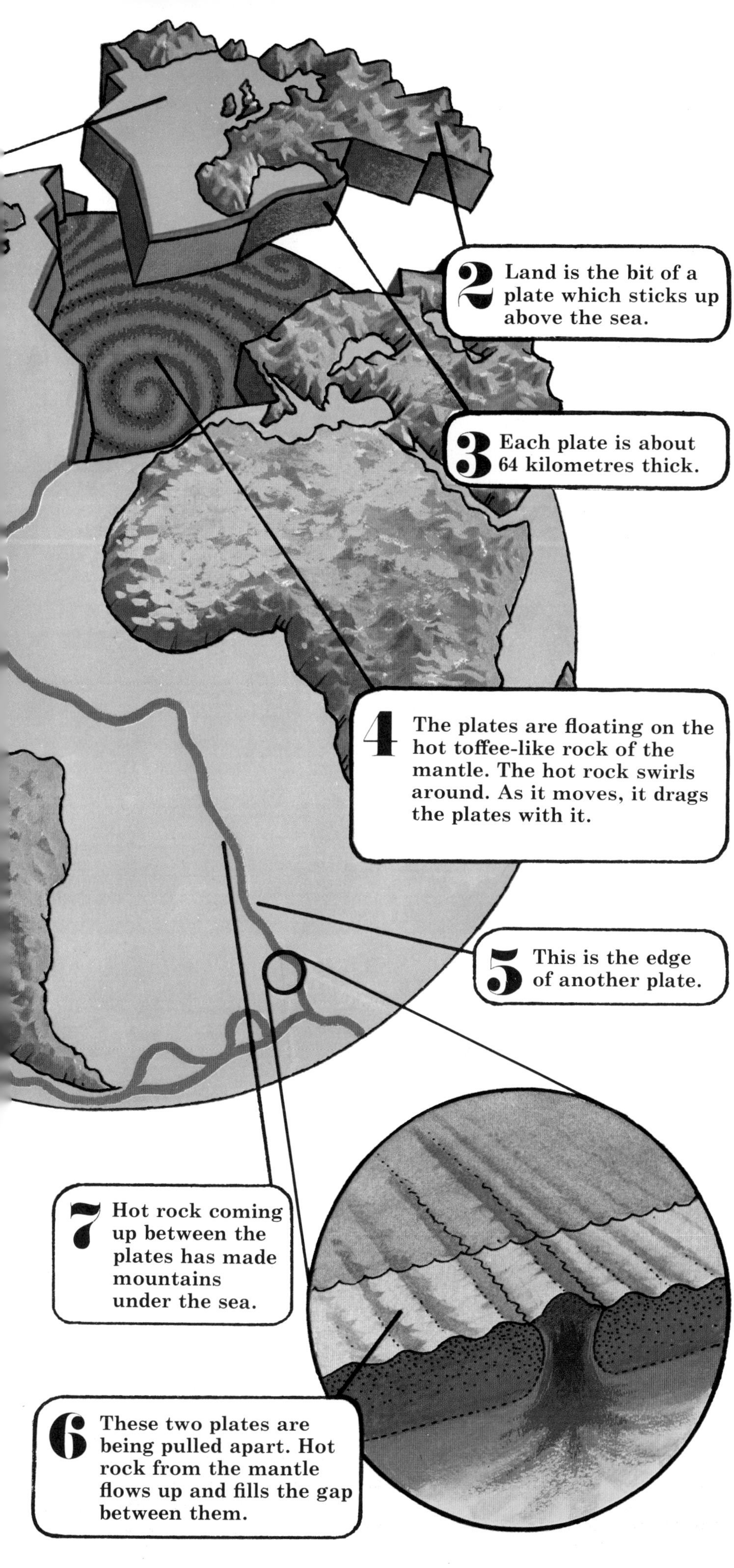

2 Land is the bit of a plate which sticks up above the sea.
3 Each plate is about 64 kilometres thick.
4 The plates are floating on the hot toffee-like rock of the mantle. The hot rock swirls around. As it moves, it drags the plates with it.
5 This is the edge of another plate.
7 Hot rock coming up between the plates has made mountains under the sea.
6 These two plates are being pulled apart. Hot rock from the mantle flows up and fills the gap between them.

Building mountains

The remains of sea creatures have been found in rocks in the Himalayan mountains. Tremendous forces must have pushed these rocks up from under the sea.

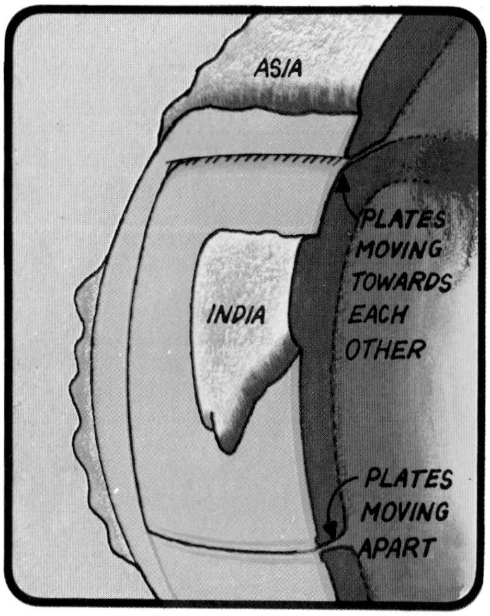

There used to be sea where the Himalayan mountains are. This was about 150 million years ago when India was being carried on its plate towards Asia.

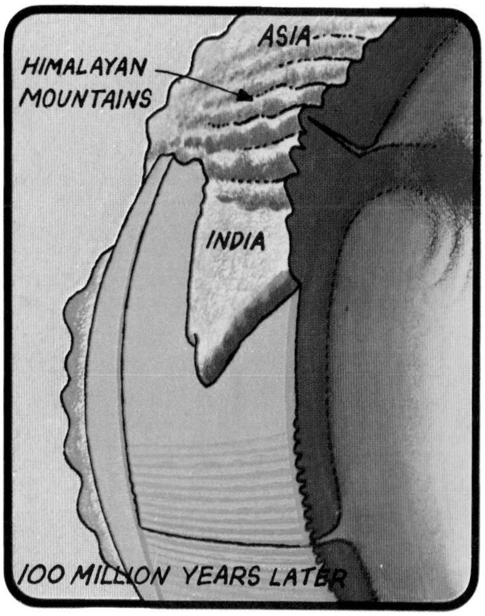

Eventually, India bumped into Asia. The rocks under the sea between them were squeezed up to make gigantic mountains. These are the Himalayan mountains.

Rocks and Fossils

As soon as the Earth's rocky crust hardened, it began to wear away. Rain and wind attacked the rock and slowly broke it into bits of sand and mud. Rock is being worn away like this all the time. Over millions of years, high mountains become low hills.

The world would be a very flat place by now if no new rocks were being made. Some new rocks are made from bits of old rock. Others are made from the liquid rock inside the Earth.

Rain, wind and ice are wearing away the rocks. This is called *weathering*. Little bits of rock break off high mountains and make them sharp and jagged.

Rain washes the bits of rock into streams. They tumble and knock against each other in the water. This grinds them down into sand and mud and little stones.

Streams and rivers carry the sand and mud all the way to the sea. Thick layers of it slowly build up on the sea floor, along with bones and shells of sea creatures.

The muddy sand is packed down by the weight of more layers piling on top. It is pressed so hard that it becomes solid rock. Rock made like this is called *sedimentary rock*.

Some of the sedimentary rock made under the sea becomes dry land. Movements in the Earth's crust lift and bend the layers of rock and make it into new hills.

Rocks from inside the Earth

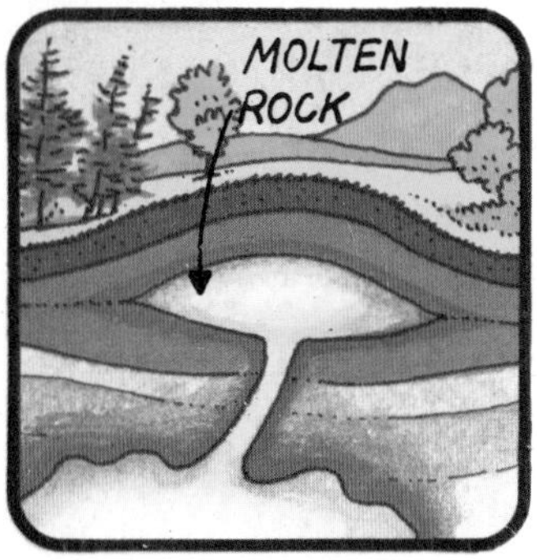

Sometimes liquid rock from inside the Earth pushes its way into the crust. It may even break right through the crust and make a volcano. When this rock cools, it hardens and is called *igneous rock*.

A common igneous rock is granite.

Molten rock in the crust heats the rocks around it and changes them. They are then called *metamorphic rocks*. Slate is one of these.

Looking at rocks

A good place to look at rocks is in cliffs or in a road cutting. If you travel by train, look in railway cuttings too. You can often see layers in the rock and find places where these layers have been bent or broken. Here are some points to look for.

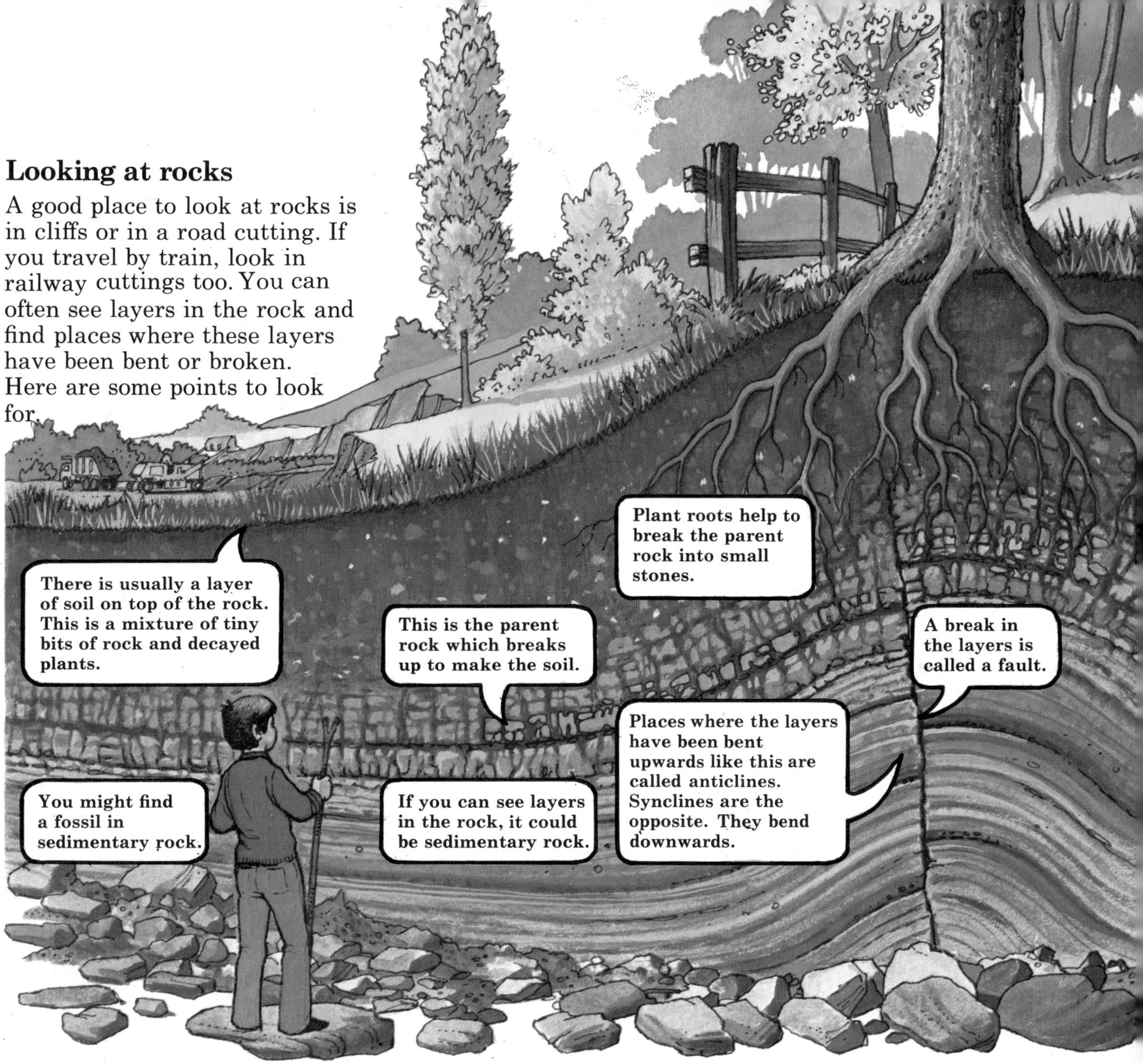

Plant roots help to break the parent rock into small stones.
There is usually a layer of soil on top of the rock. This is a mixture of tiny bits of rock and decayed plants.
This is the parent rock which breaks up to make the soil.
A break in the layers is called a fault.
Places where the layers have been bent upwards like this are called anticlines. Synclines are the opposite. They bend downwards.
You might find a fossil in sedimentary rock.
If you can see layers in the rock, it could be sedimentary rock.

Fossils

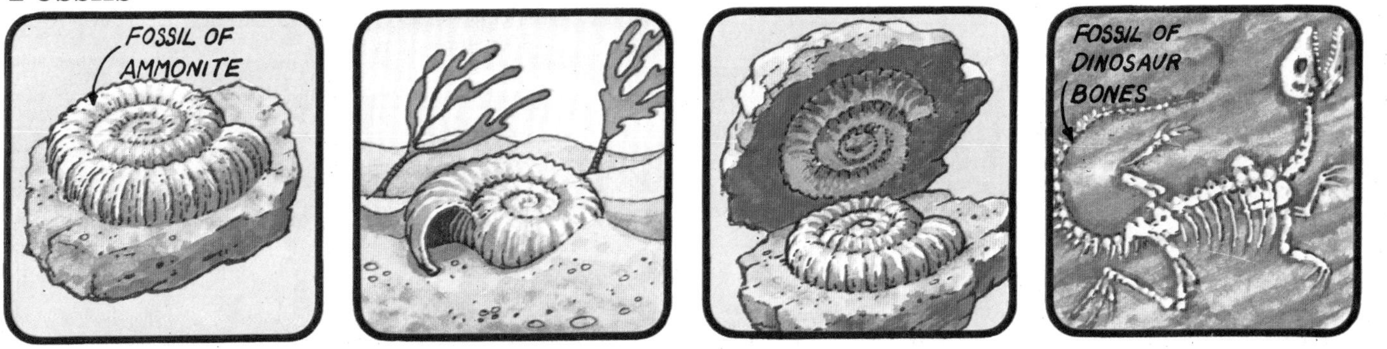

FOSSIL OF AMMONITE
FOSSIL OF DINOSAUR BONES

Shapes of animals and plants which lived millions of years ago are sometimes found in sedimentary rocks. These are *fossils*. This is the fossil of an ammonite, a sea creature which lived at the same time as dinosaurs.

When the ammonite died, its shell was covered with sand and mud. This was all pressed down and the rock that formed had a pattern, or fossil, of the shell in it. Fossils tell us a lot about plants and animals that lived long ago.

The Earth in Space

Your address in space

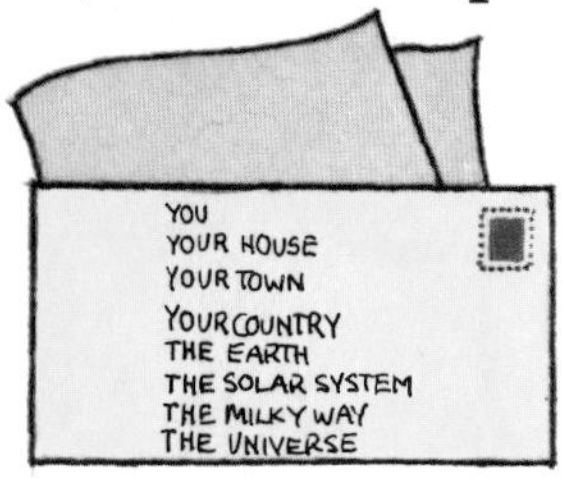

It is difficult to imagine how big space is. Our Earth is just one of millions of objects floating around in it. Most of these objects are *stars* —balls of hot gas which give out heat and light. Some are so far away that it would take millions of years to reach them.

These pictures show where you fit in the universe. Imagine you are writing your address in space. This is you in your house and your house in your street.

Your house is a small part of a town, so you write the name of your town next.

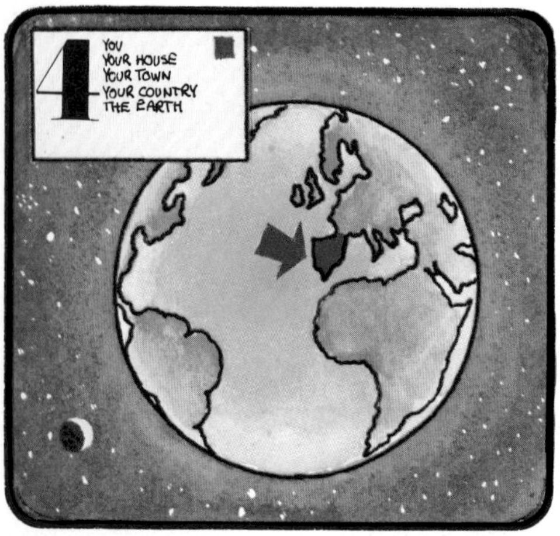

Your country is just a little bit of the land on the Earth. Land covers less than one-third of the Earth's surface. The rest is covered by sea.

The Earth is one of nine *planets* going round a star which we call the Sun. Together they are known as the *solar system.* Planets do not give out light like stars.

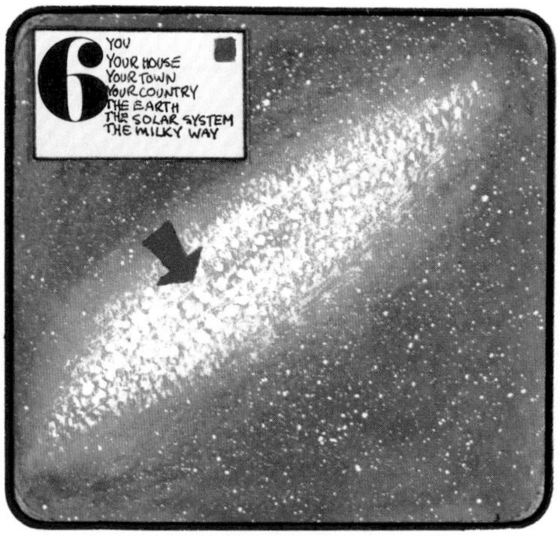

The solar system belongs to a group of 100,000 million stars called the Milky Way. This is our *galaxy.* On a clear night you can see it as a hazy glow in the sky.

The Moon

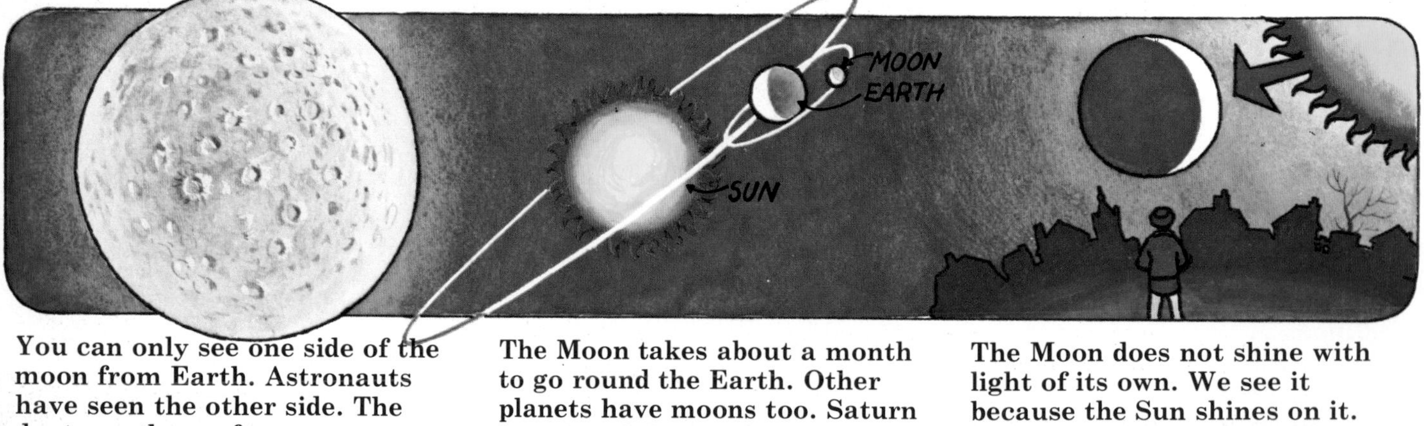

You can only see one side of the moon from Earth. Astronauts have seen the other side. The dents on the surface are craters.

The Moon takes about a month to go round the Earth. Other planets have moons too. Saturn has 10 and Jupiter has 13.

The Moon does not shine with light of its own. We see it because the Sun shines on it. Often part of it is in shadow.

This is your town in your country. Your town probably seems quite large. When you see it surrounded by other towns and countryside, it does not seem so big.

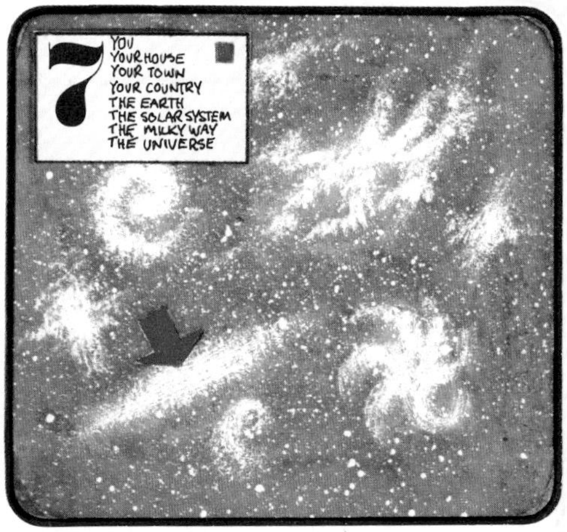

There are millions of galaxies in the universe. They are not all the same size or shape as our own. Some may contain planets like ours, but we do not know.

The planets

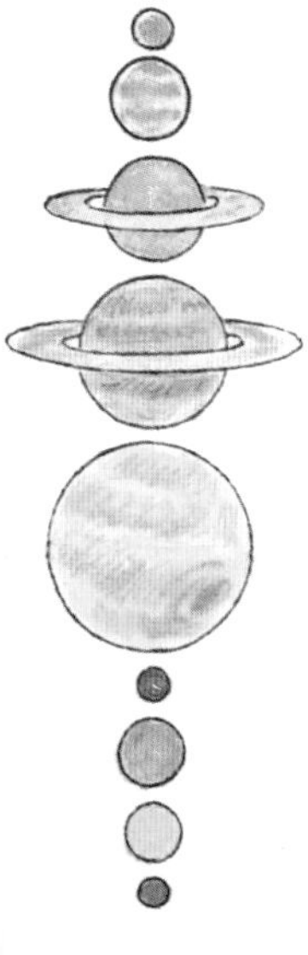

Pluto. Dark and cold.
Neptune. Giant, greeny-blue planet.

Uranus. Five moons. Rings discovered 1977.

Saturn. Big rings, probably made of dust and ice.

Jupiter. Largest planet in the solar system. One ring of rocky debris.
Mars. Called the Red Planet as it is made of red rock.
Earth. Has one moon.

Venus. Hottest planet.
Mercury. Next to Sun.

Day and night

The Earth is spinning round all the time, though you cannot feel it. It takes 24 hours to spin round once.

Think of one place and follow it as the Earth goes round. For about 12 hours it is in light from the Sun. This is its day. Then it moves into the shadow behind the Earth and it is night for 12 hours.

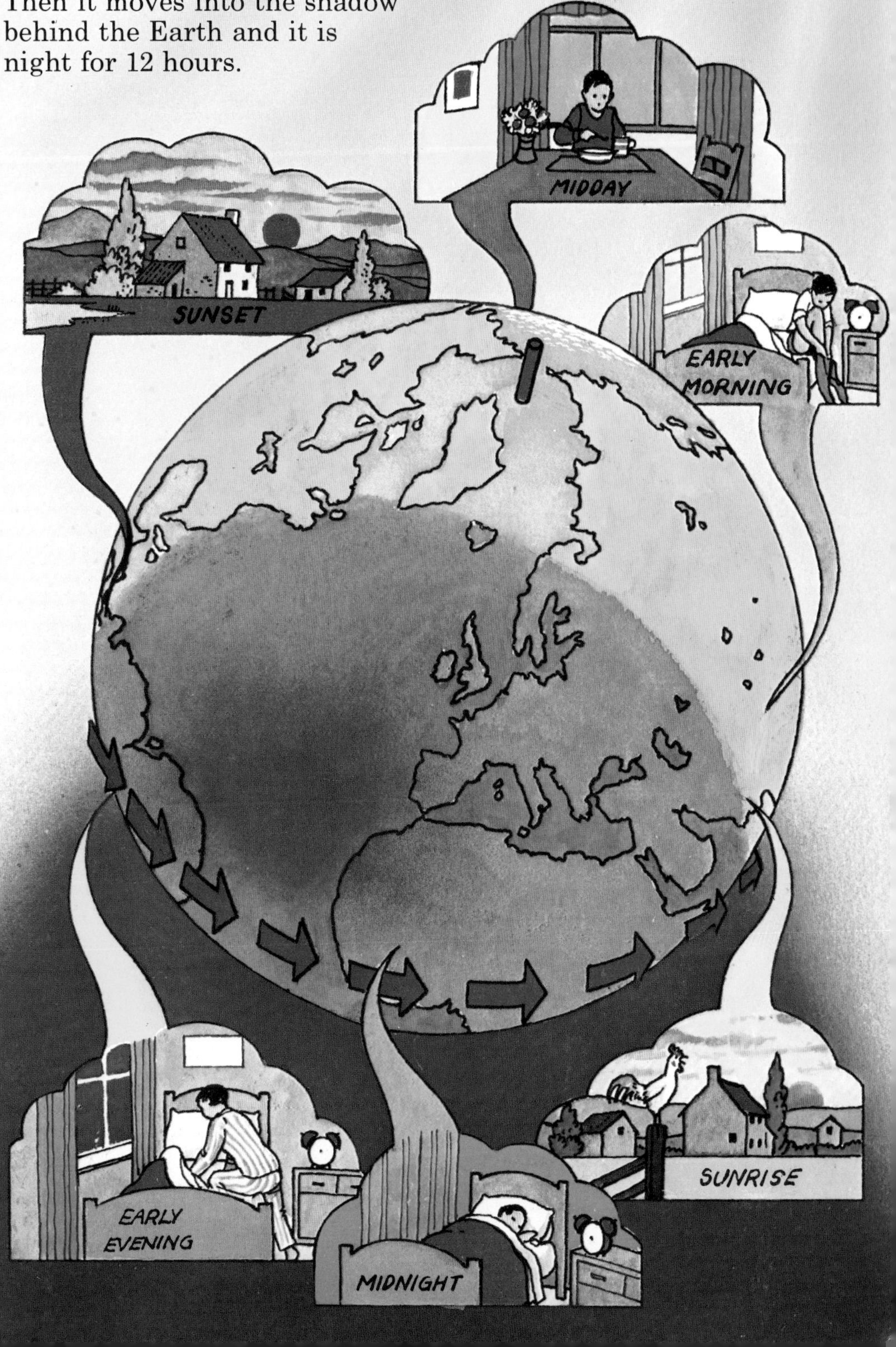

Summer and Winter

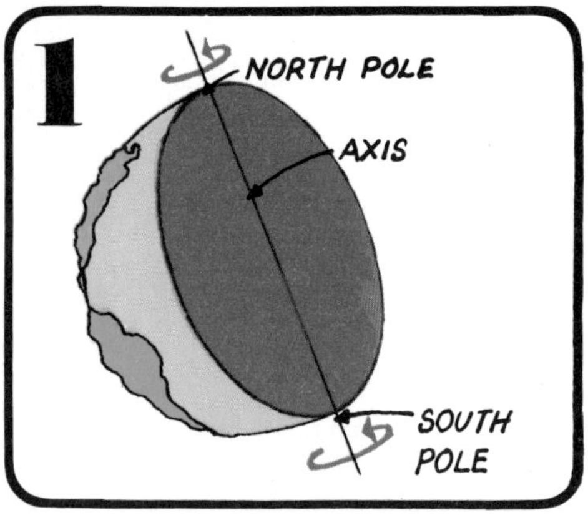

Before we can explain the seasons properly, we need to tell you some words to do with the Earth. First, there is the *axis*. This is the line through the middle of the Earth.

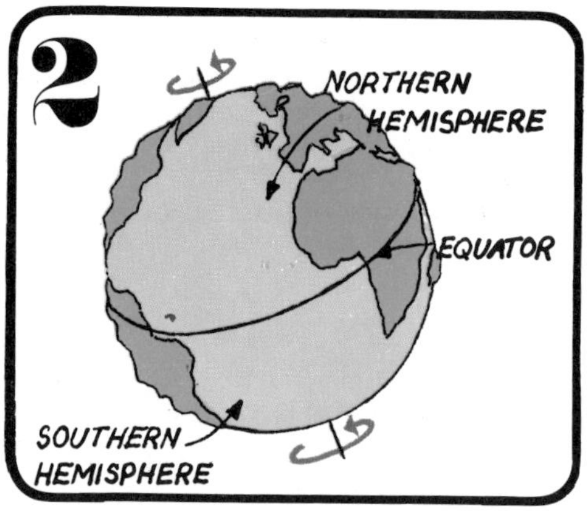

The *equator* is a line round the widest part of the Earth. The top half of the Earth is the *northern hemisphere* and the bottom half is the *southern hemisphere*.

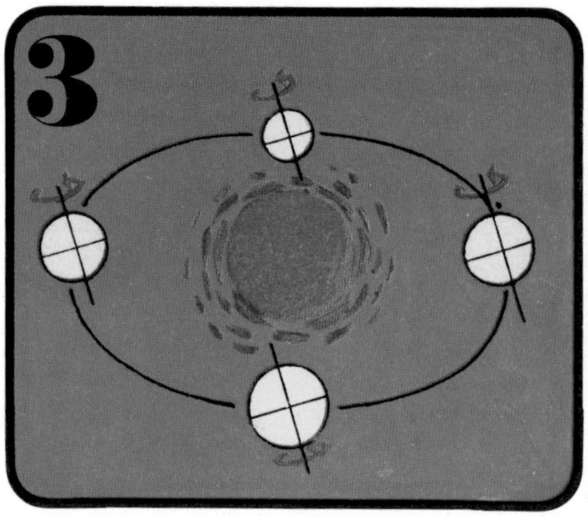

The seasons change because the Earth's axis leans over to one side. On the Earth's trip round the Sun, first one hemisphere and then the other is closer to the Sun.

How the seasons change

Summer happens in the hemisphere that is closer to the Sun. It is winter in the other hemisphere. Follow the Earth round the Sun and see how the seasons change.

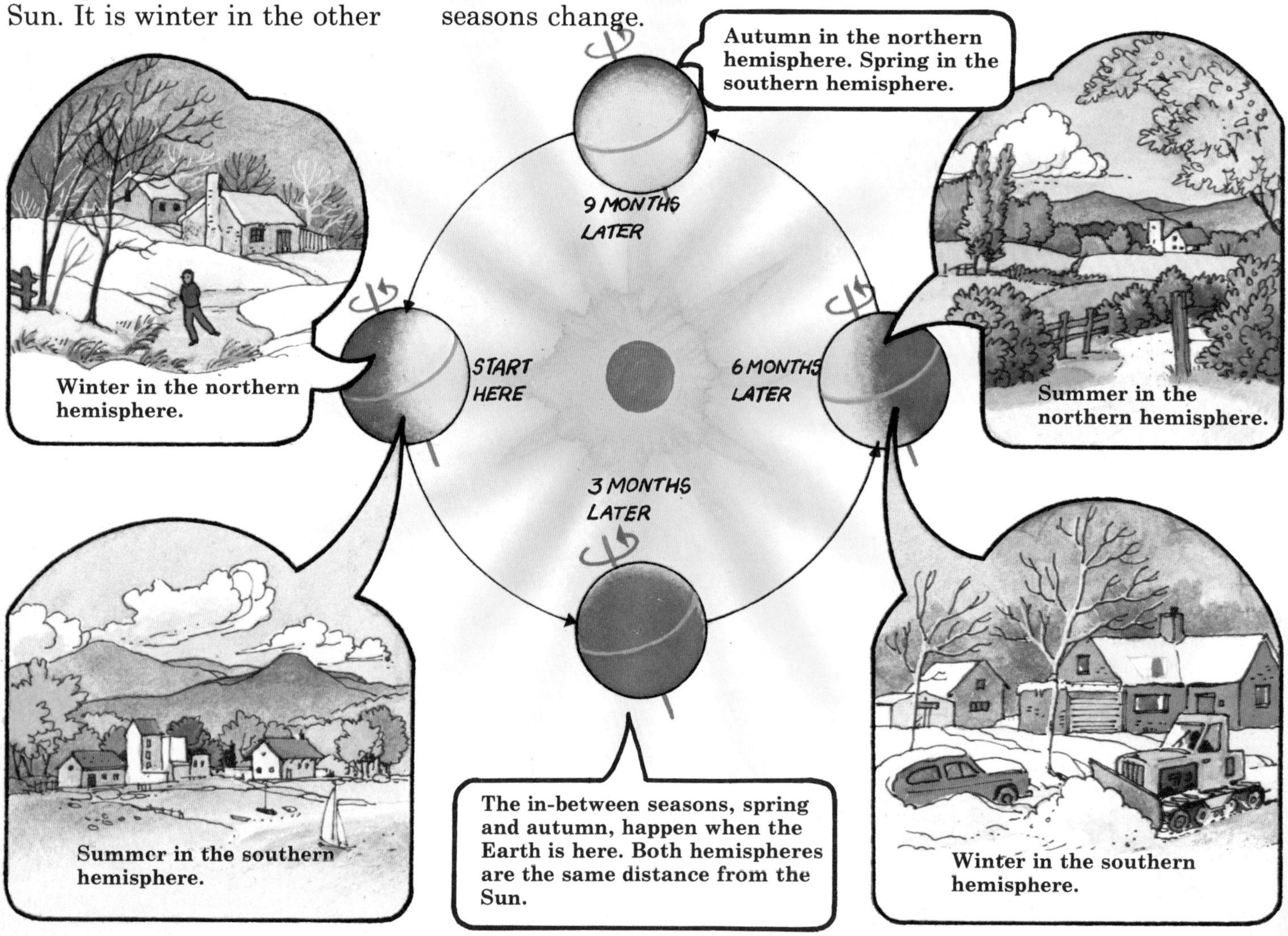

Autumn in the northern hemisphere. Spring in the southern hemisphere.
9 MONTHS LATER
START HERE
6 MONTHS LATER
3 MONTHS LATER
Winter in the northern hemisphere.
Summer in the northern hemisphere.
Summer in the southern hemisphere.
The in-between seasons, spring and autumn, happen when the Earth is here. Both hemispheres are the same distance from the Sun.
Winter in the southern hemisphere.

The Sky

The Earth is wrapped in a blanket of air called the *atmosphere*. This gets thinner and thinner as you move away from the Earth. There is no air at all beyond about 550 km, which is where the atmosphere ends and space begins.

The air is a mixture of gases. One of them is oxygen which we must breathe to stay alive. Another is carbon dioxide which plants need. There is also water in the air.

Most of our weather is made in the bottom 15 km of the atmosphere, so this is the bit we have shown here.

The highest clouds you can see are cirrus clouds. The air is very cold at this height and these clouds are made of little bits of ice.
There is very little air at the height at which jet planes fly. Air is pumped into the cabin for the passengers to breathe.
The air at this height is colder than the air at sea level, so high mountains are always covered with snow.
When there is a lot of water in the air, you can see it as clouds.
Mountaineers carry oxygen in tanks on their backs when they climb very high. This is because there is not enough oxygen in the air for them to breathe.
There is more water in the air near the Earth, so the clouds there are bigger than those higher up.
Wind is just the air moving around.
Carbon dioxide is the gas in the air that plants need so that they can grow.
The air is like a blanket round the Earth. It keeps it warm at night. During the day, it protects us from the Sun's rays. We would be burnt to cinders if it were not there.
The air is heavy. The weight of it pressing down on your head is about 100 kg.

Where Rain comes from

Rain is not new water. The water which falls as rain comes from the sea, the rivers, the lakes and even from wet clothes hanging on washing lines.

These pictures show how this water becomes drops of rain or even snow flakes.

When washing dries the water does not just disappear. It becomes part of the air. Water in the air is called *water vapour*.

We say water is evaporating when it changes into water vapour. Water is evaporating from the sea, from lakes and from rivers nearly all the time.

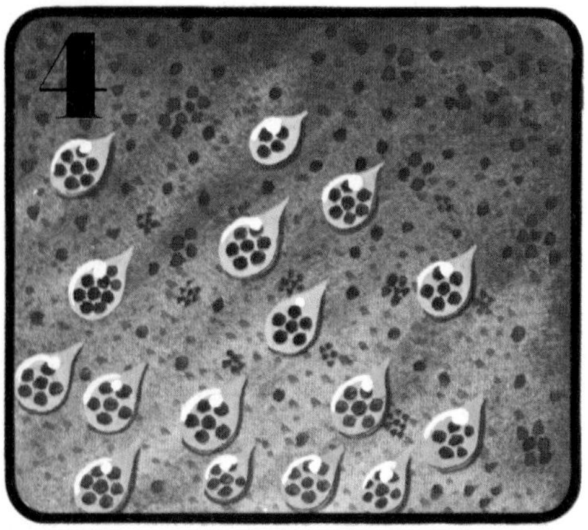

Thousands of cloud droplets join to make one rain drop. Scientists are not sure how this happens. They think perhaps the droplets collect round a speck of dust.

If it is very cold, the cloud droplets stick together and make snow flakes. Snow flakes are lots of different shapes, but each one has six sides.

Snow flakes sometimes melt and become rain before they reach the ground. Sometimes they half-melt and fall as icy rain called *sleet*.

Thunder and lightning

Thunder storm clouds are very tall, puffy and dark. Lightning is a huge spark of electricity in the clouds and thunder is the noise made by this spark.

Thunder and lightning happen at the same time. You hear the thunder after you have seen the lightning because sound travels more slowly than light.

Try counting the seconds between the lightning and the thunder. Divide this by three to work out how far away the storm is in kilometres.

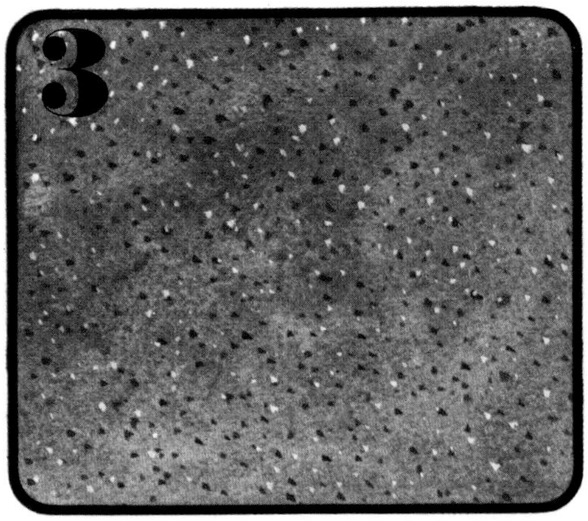

When the air gets colder, the vapour changes into minute droplets of water. These droplets are not heavy enough to fall as rain. They hang in the air as cloud.

Weather forecasting

This is the weather satellite, NOAA. It is a spacecraft which goes round the Earth and takes photographs of it from 1,500 km out in space. These photographs show the clouds covering the Earth. By studying them, weathermen can tell what our weather will be like.

WINGS MAKE ELECTRICITY FROM THE SUNLIGHT TO POWER THE SATELLITE

How to be a weather forecaster

You can get an idea of what the weather will be like by looking at the clouds.

Use this guide to help you identify the clouds in the sky. Later, note the weather they have made. You will soon know what weather to expect from different clouds.

Cirrus clouds. Very high and wispy. Warmer weather coming.
Cirrocumulus. Bands of puffy cloud across the sky. Rain coming soon.
Altocumulus. Small, puffy, white clouds high in the sky. It may rain tomorrow.
Thunder clouds. Wider at the top than the bottom. Thunder and heavy rain coming.
Tall cumulus clouds. Heavy rain very soon.
Flat cumulus clouds. Warm sunny day.
Nimbostratus. Grey cloud covering whole sky. Probably drizzle and rain soon.
Fog is cloud very near the ground.

Underground Caves

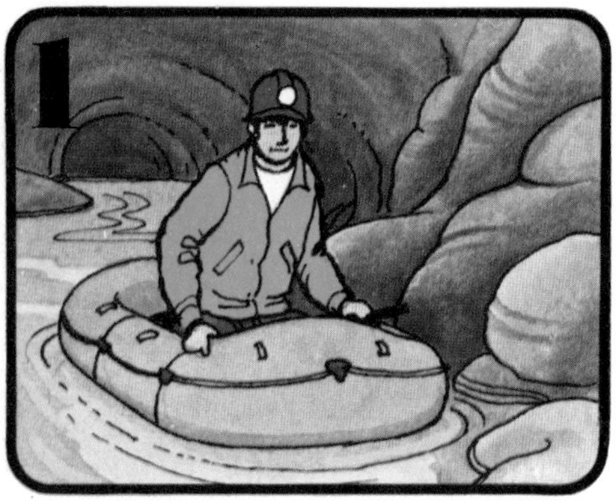

In some places there are huge caves and tunnels under the ground. They are usually found where the rock is *limestone*, because it is easily worn away.

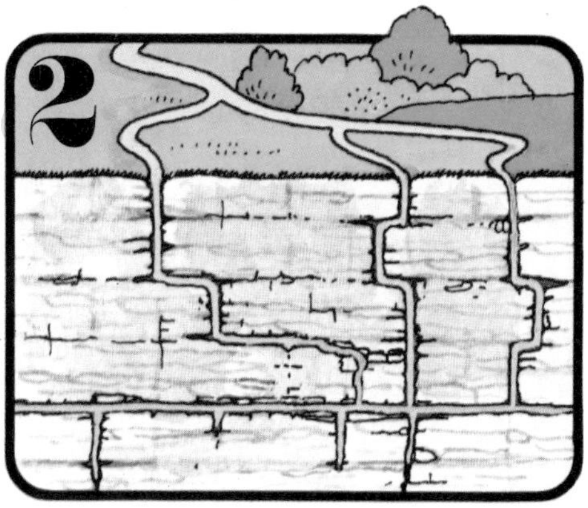

Limestone is a sedimentary rock, so it is made up of layers. There are cracks where the layers have broken. Water trickles down these and along between the layers.

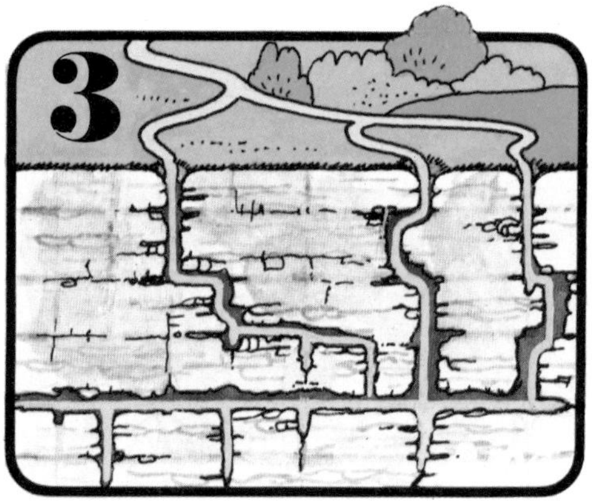

Limestone rock dissolves in water rather like a sugar lump does, only much more slowly. So as the water trickles through the rock it widens the cracks.

Going underground

Here are some underground caves and tunnels for you to explore.

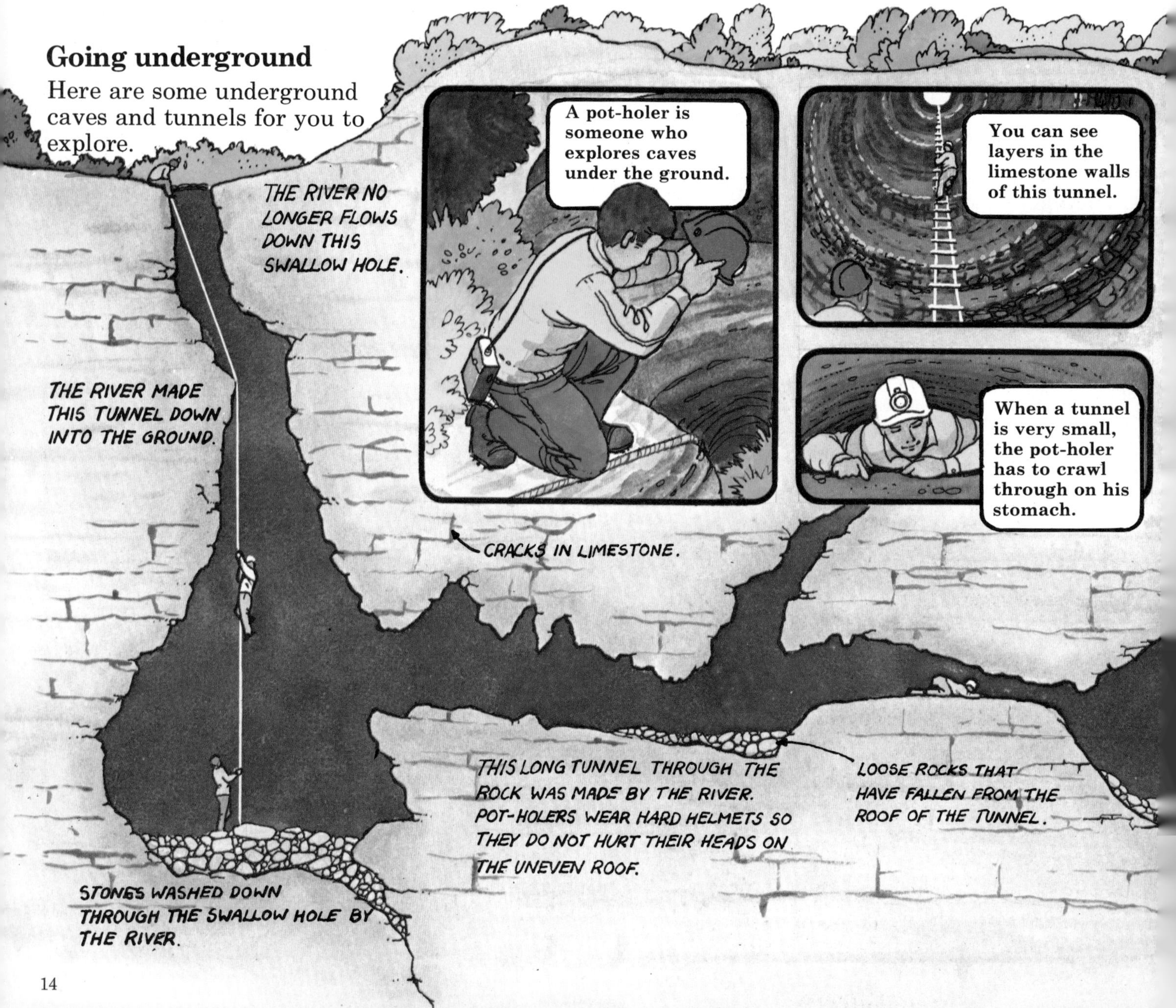

A pot-holer is someone who explores caves under the ground.
You can see layers in the limestone walls of this tunnel.
When a tunnel is very small, the pot-holer has to crawl through on his stomach.
THE RIVER NO LONGER FLOWS DOWN THIS SWALLOW HOLE.
THE RIVER MADE THIS TUNNEL DOWN INTO THE GROUND.
CRACKS IN LIMESTONE.
THIS LONG TUNNEL THROUGH THE ROCK WAS MADE BY THE RIVER. POT-HOLERS WEAR HARD HELMETS SO THEY DO NOT HURT THEIR HEADS ON THE UNEVEN ROOF.
LOOSE ROCKS THAT HAVE FALLEN FROM THE ROOF OF THE TUNNEL.
STONES WASHED DOWN THROUGH THE SWALLOW HOLE BY THE RIVER.

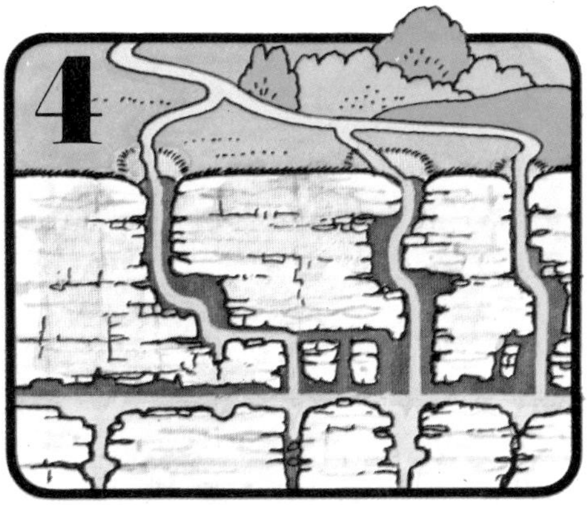

Eventually the cracks become wide tunnels and a river might flow down through them. The place where a river goes into the ground is called a *swallow hole*.

The river may flow for many kilometres under the ground. It dissolves away more of the limestone and makes the long tunnels and caves in the rock.

Water drips from the cave roof and leaves behind some of the limstone which was dissolved in it. This grows down and makes a *stalactite*.
Water with limestone dissolved in it drips on to the cave floor and makes *stalagmites.*
Pillars are made when stalactites and stalagmites join up.
STALACTITES ARE FINGERS OF ROCK HANGING FROM THE CAVE ROOF. REMEMBER THEIR NAME BY THINKING "STALACTITES HAVE TO HOLD ON TIGHT"
STALAGMITES ARE MOUNDS OF ROCK ON THE CAVE FLOOR.
POT-HOLERS OFTEN CARRY INFLATABLE RUBBER DINGHIES IN CASE THEY FIND AN UNDERGROUND LAKE LIKE THIS ONE.

Discovering caves

On September 12, 1940, four boys went out hunting. They lost their dog, Robot, but they could hear him barking in a hole in the ground.

The boys climbed down the hole to rescue Robot. They found themselves in a huge cave with paintings of animals on the walls and ceiling.

The cave the boys discovered is in Lascaux, France. The paintings were done 15,000 years ago by cavemen.

Useful Things from the Ground

The first people made tools and weapons out of stone. Later, they discovered how to get iron from rocks and make metal tools. Now people dig mines and quarries for all sorts of different rocks and metals.

Coal is a useful rock because it gives out a lot of heat when it burns. It is called a *fossil fuel* because it is made from fossilized plants. Another fossil fuel is oil, which is made from tiny sea creatures. Chemicals, candles, tar, plastics and nylon are made from oil.

Coal is made of trees which lived about 300 million years ago. The land was wet and swampy then, and covered with thick forests of trees.

The swamps were full of leaves and dead branches from the trees. The water in the swamps was very acid and this stopped the wood from rotting.

Later, the swampy land was flooded by the sea. A thick layer of sand settled at the bottom of the sea and covered the dead trees.

The dead wood was packed down very hard by the weight of the sand on top of it. Slowly it hardened to form coal.

Tunnels are dug through the ground to reach the coal, which is in layers called seams. Powerful machines cut out the coal and make tunnels in the seam.

How oil is made

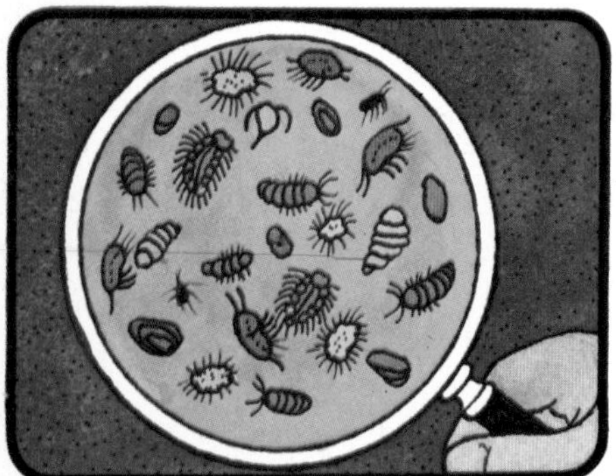

Scientists think that oil is made from tiny sea creatures like these. When these creatures die they fall to the sea floor and are buried in mud.

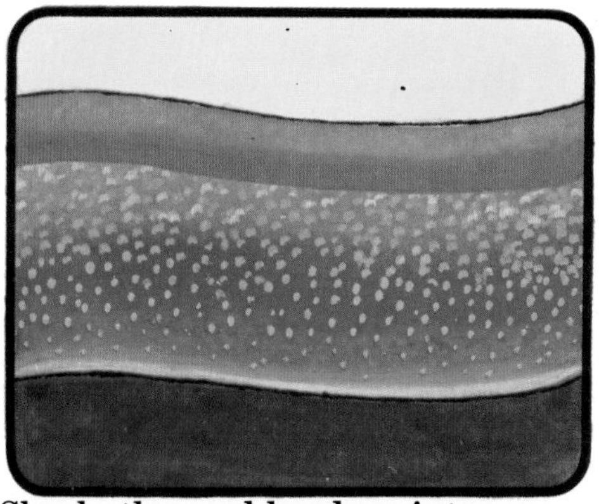

Slowly the mud hardens into rock and the creatures inside it change into little drops of oil. This takes millions of years.

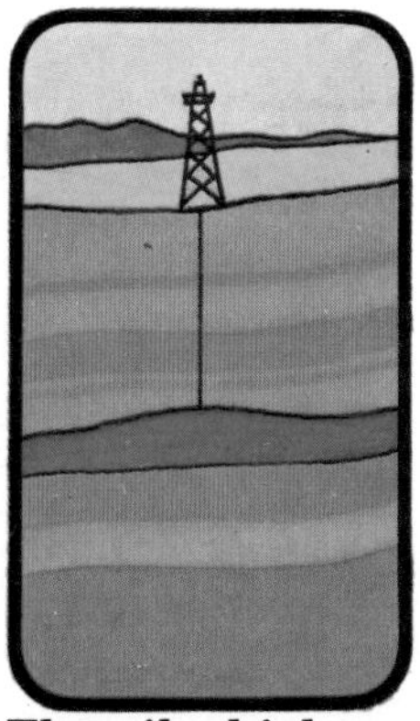

The oil which comes out of the ground is called crude oil. This is piped to refineries where it is separated into petrol and other oils.

What Happens in an Earthquake

September 1, 1923, was a hot, clear day in Tokyo, the capital city of Japan. Towards the middle of the morning people were hurrying home for lunch.

Suddenly the ground began to tremble and shake and huge cracks opened in it. People running for safety were buried as houses fell down.

Gas pipes broke and fire quickly spread through the town. Fire often causes as much damage in an earthquake as the shaking of the ground.

More than 140,000 people were killed in this earthquake. Most of them were burnt to death. Others drowned when an enormous wave flooded the ruined city.

Why earthquakes happen

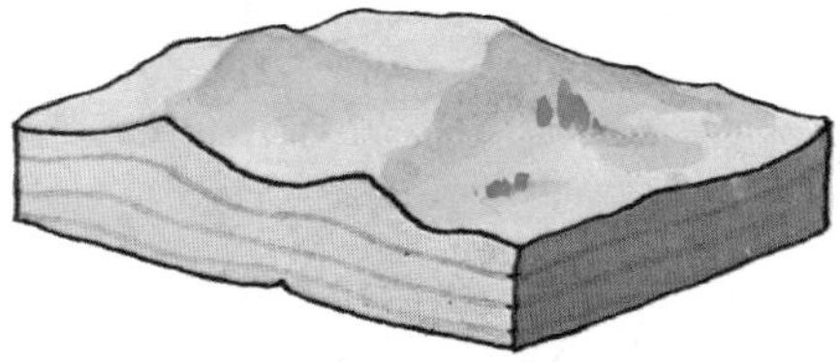

Rock looks hard and brittle, but when it is under a lot of weight it will bend a bit. In parts of the Earth's crust there are strong forces slowly bending the rock.

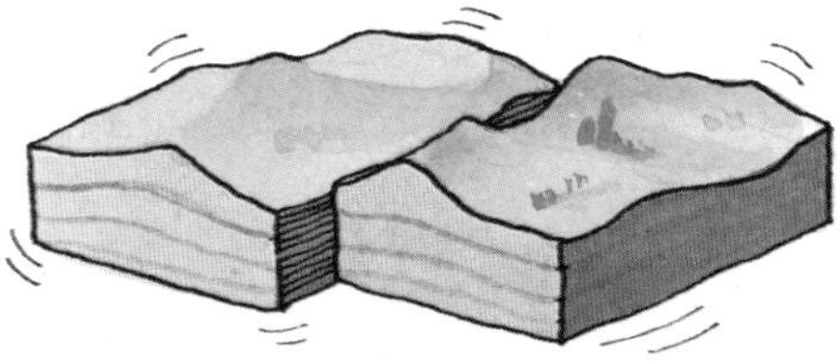

When the rock is bent too much, it suddenly snaps and the two pieces shudder and move a bit. The rocks above shake and we feel it as an *earthquake.*

Hot water from the ground

If there are hot rocks in the Earth's crust, they heat the underground water. Sometimes hot water spurts out of the ground. This is a *geyser*.

This steaming hot spring bubbles out of the ground in Iceland. Hot water is piped straight from this river to houses in the nearby town.

Volcanoes

On February 20, 1943, a Mexican farmer called Dionisio was ploughing his field. He heard strange rumbling noises and stopped. Then he saw smoke coming out of the ground.

Dionisio dropped his tools and ran. Next morning, frightened people from his village saw a smoking heap of ash in the field. It was already five times as high as a man.

The heap grew. By the end of the week it was 150 metres high. Hot stones, ash and steam were shooting out of the top.

A volcano cut in half

In some places the Earth's crust is thin or cracked. Here, the hot, liquid rock inside the Earth is able to force its way through the crust and form *volcanoes*.

Sometimes the hot, molten rock seeps out slowly. Sometimes there are lots of gases in the hot rock and it explodes through the crust very violently.

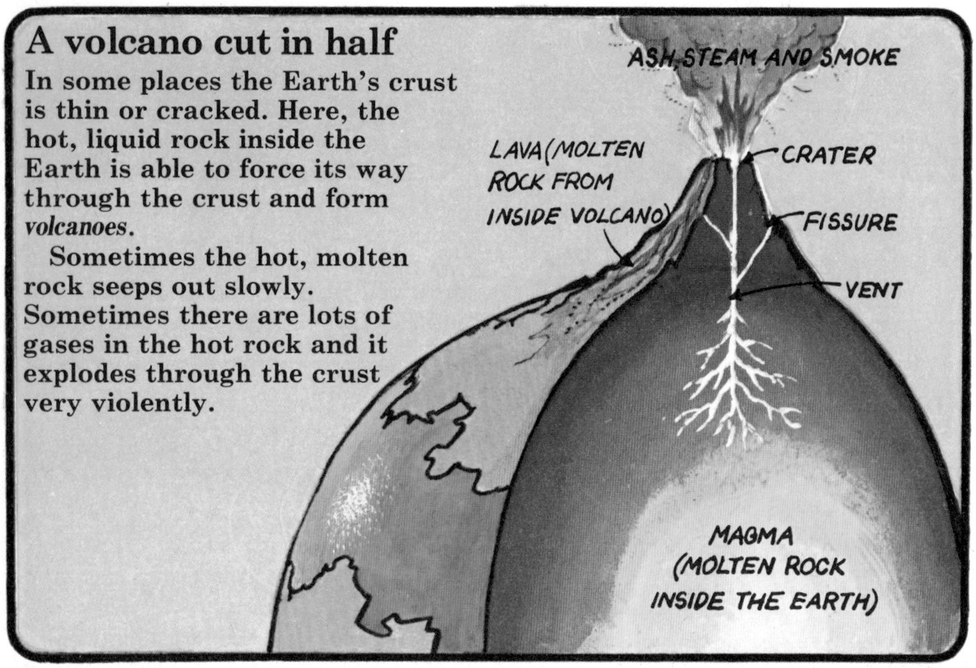

Looking inside

Scientists sometimes go down inside volcanoes to find out more about them. They wear suits made of fibre-glass and aluminium to protect them from the heat.

A buried town

Mount Vesuvius in Italy had been quiet for hundreds of years. Suddenly on August 24, AD 79 it erupted violently. The nearby town of Pompeii was buried in hot lava before the people had time to get away.

Historians have dug up the remains of the town. They found body-shaped holes where the people's bodies had lain before they decayed.

This plaster cast was made by pouring plaster into the body-shaped holes.

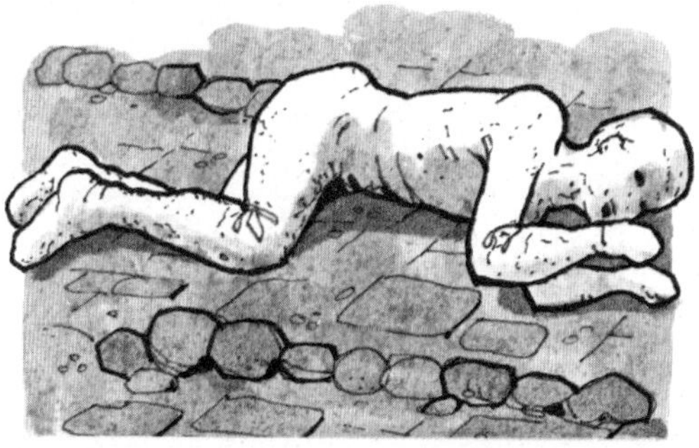

Bread, eggs and nuts were found in the remains of the town. They had been preserved by the lava.

Red-hot, liquid rock, called lava, poured out of the volcano. It buried buildings and set fire to trees. Dionisio's village was completely destroyed.

This volcano was named Paricutin, after Dionisio's village. A year later its lava buried a nearby town. Only the church tower was left sticking up above the lava.

How a new island was made

Volcanoes sometimes erupt in the sea. In 1963 some fishermen saw smoke rising out of the sea near Iceland. Then the top of a volcano appeared above the water. Red-hot lava poured out and it looked like a glowing fire in the sea. The volcano slowly cooled down. The new island was named Surtsey. Birds began to nest on it. Plants grew from seeds dropped by birds or washed up by the sea.

The Journey of a River

Rivers make valleys in the hills and help shape the countryside. Their water comes from rain and melted snow. If there is not much rain, the rivers dry up.

Follow this river on its journey from the hills to the sea and find out what happens to it on the way.

Rain water drains into streams.
Lots of streams join to make a river.
The place where a river begins is called its source.
This is a spur. Look at picture ① on the left to find out more about it.
Some rain water soaks through the ground and bubbles out as a spring many kilometres away.

A river does not flow straight. It swings from side to side and cuts a winding valley. The pieces of hill sticking out across the valley are called *spurs*.

Some waterfalls are made when a river flows over a hard rock onto a softer one. The softer rock wears away and makes a step. The water then tumbles over the step.

Loops in the river are called *meanders*. After a while, the river may break its banks and flow straight on. The loop it leaves behind is called an *ox-bow lake*.

A river which flows into another river is called a tributary.

Water in the ground

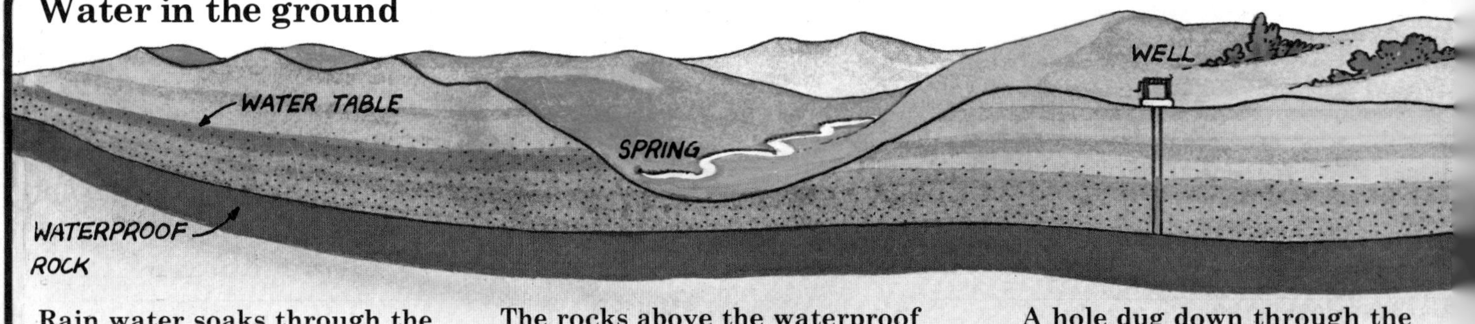

Rain water soaks through the ground until it reaches a waterproof rock. This sort of rock is too solid for water to trickle through.

The rocks above the waterproof rock hold water rather like a sponge does. The top of the water in them is called the *water table*.

A hole dug down through the water table soon fills with water This is how a well is made.

The place where a river flows into the sea is called its mouth.
The river drops all of its load of sand and mud when it flows into the sea. If the sea does not wash it away it builds up to make a *delta* like this.
This is a meander. Find out more about it from picture 3 on the left.
When the river floods, it spreads mud over the land. This makes good soil for plants to grow in.
Look at picture 2 to find out how a waterfall is made.
The river flows more slowly on flatter land and drops some of the stones it is carrying.
A river carries lots of stones, sand and mud in its water. This is called its load.

OASIS

There is water under the ground even in the desert. If there is a dip in the ground and the water table is near the surface, it makes an *oasis*.

Power from rivers

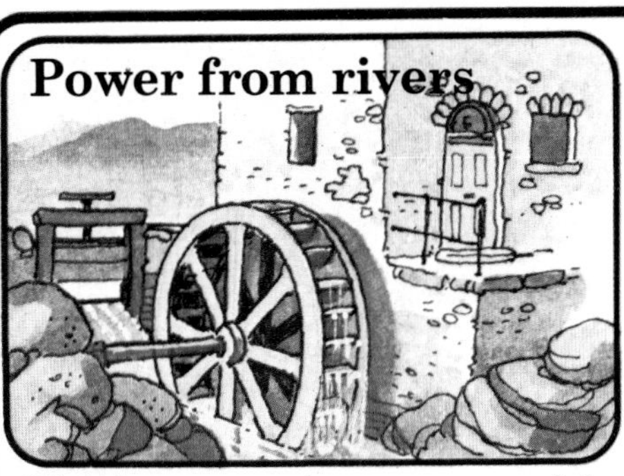

Flowing water is very powerful. People used to build mills by rivers and use the water to turn a mill wheel. This drove the machinery for grinding corn.

Water can be used to drive the machines which make electricity. A river is dammed and the water is piped to the power station.

Going up a Mountain

As you climb higher up a mountain you feel colder and colder. Even in very hot places, you will find snow on the mountains if you climb high enough.

Winter high in the mountains is bitterly cold. The ground is covered with snow for most of the year. Only special mountain plants that can stand the cold are able to grow there.

Follow the climber in these pictures and see how the mountainside changes as you climb higher.

The kind of trees that grow furthest up a mountain are *conifers*. They have stiff, needle-shaped leaves which help the trees survive the cold weather.

Suddenly, the trees end. They do not grow further up the mountain because it is too cold. This height is called the *tree line*. Above it, there is only grass.

Hollows high up in the mountains are full of deep snow.
Snow packs down and changes to solid ice as all the air is squeezed out.
The ice is pushed down the mountain as more ice is made behind it.
Most glaciers move only a few centimetres a day.
Stones which fall on the glacier are carried down the mountain and are called *moraine.*
A split in the ice is called a crevasse. Some are over 30 metres deep.
The glacier melts as it gets warmer further down the mountain.
The end of the glacier is called its snout.
Water from melting ice makes a new river.

A glacier

A *glacier* is a solid mass of ice which moves very slowly down the mountain. It is made from the deep snow at the top of the mountain.

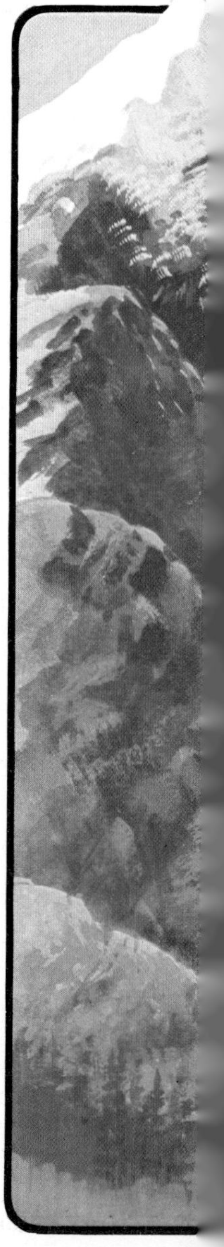

Higher up still, the mountain is rocky and bare. The air feels cold and there are patches of snow even in summer. Tiny flowers grow during the warmer months.

Now you have reached the *snow line*. Above here the mountain is always covered with snow. The snow is very deep and nothing can grow here.

Snow slides

People who live in high mountains know that the snow may suddenly slip off the steep mountain slope. When this happens, it is called an *avalanche*.

A sudden noise or movement—somebody shouting perhaps—can start the snow slipping. Masses of snow slide down the mountain and bury everything on the way.

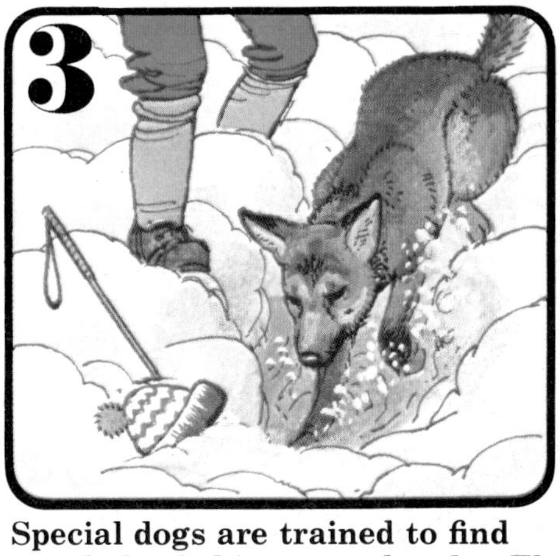

Special dogs are trained to find people buried in an avalanche. The dogs sniff the snow till they find someone. Then they dig them out with their paws.

After a glacier has melted

Thousands of years ago the weather was very cold. There were more glaciers than there are now. When the ice melted, the glaciers left valleys which looked like this.

The hollow where the glacier started is called a cirque.
The glacier carved this deep, steep-sided valley.
This valley was dug by a smaller glacier. It is not as deep as the main valley.
The river cascades over a waterfall to the main valley.
This hill is made of stones dropped by the glacier. It is called a moraine.
The moraine dammed the river so the river flooded the valley and made this lake.
Eventually the river will wear a channel through the moraine. Then the lake will drain away.

Hot and Cold Places

These pictures take you on a trip from the North Pole to the equator.

The Poles are the coldest places on Earth. As you travel down from the North Pole, each place you visit is warmer than the last. The landscape changes with the weather.

Places on the equator are always hot. After you have passed the equator, the weather begins to get cooler again. It gets colder and colder then until you reach the South Pole.

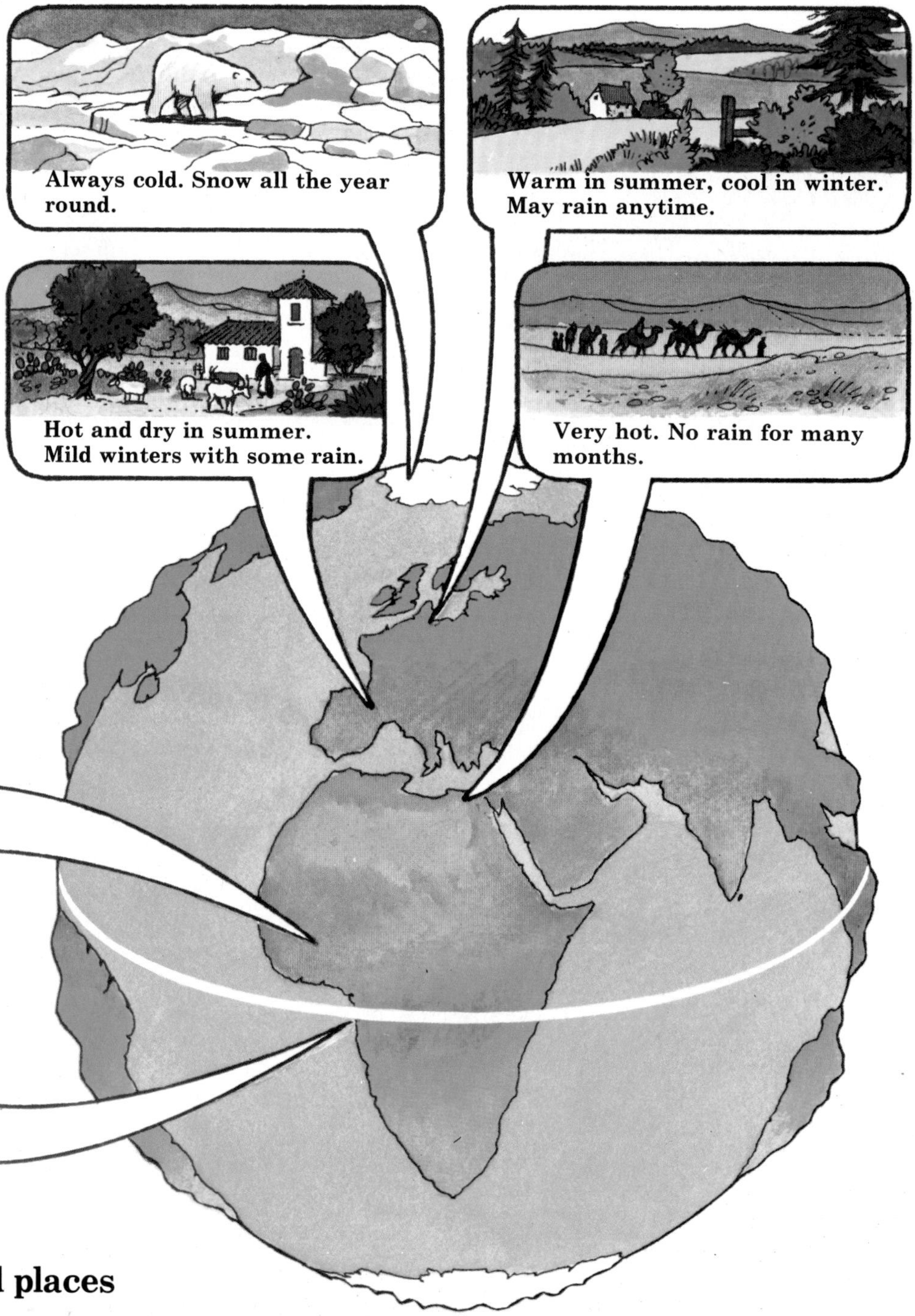

Always cold. Snow all the year round.
Warm in summer, cool in winter. May rain anytime.
Hot and dry in summer. Mild winters with some rain.
Very hot. No rain for many months.

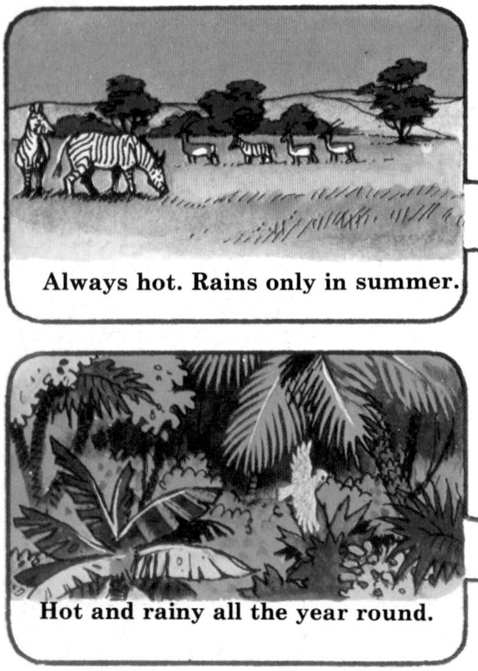

Always hot. Rains only in summer.
Hot and rainy all the year round.

Why there are hot and cold places

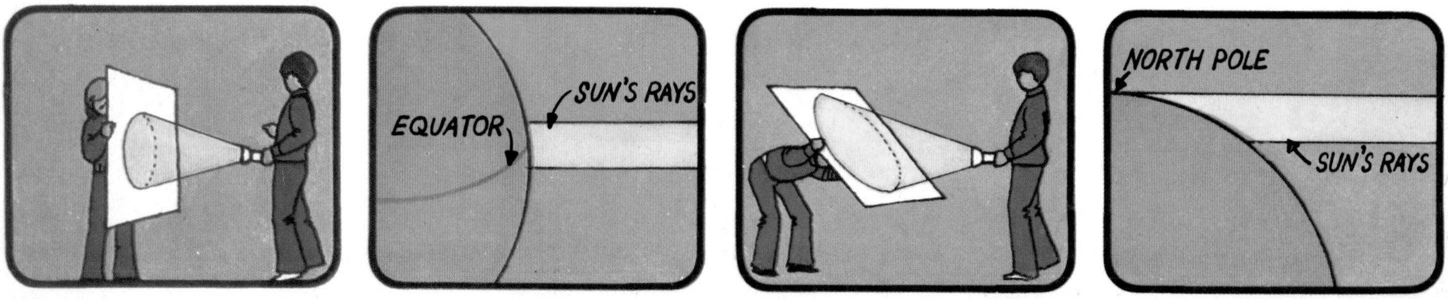

SUN'S RAYS
EQUATOR
NORTH POLE
SUN'S RAYS

A torch shining straight at a piece of card makes a small, but very bright, patch of light. The Sun's rays are like this at the equator and make it very hot there.

When the card is tilted, the patch of light is much bigger but paler. The Sun's rays are like this at the Poles. Each ray spreads out very thinly and so does not heat the land much.

Hot Dry Places

Deserts are the driest places in the world. They sometimes have no rain for several years. Cactus plants can live there because they store water in their stalks.

Not all deserts are sandy. In some, the ground is rocky with very little soil. Wind and sudden rain storms wear the rock into these strange shapes.

In a sandy desert, the wind heaps sand into little hills called *dunes*. The dunes move forward as sand is blown up the gentle slope and slips over the steep side.

There is water in the ground even though it hardly ever rains. If this water reaches the surface, it makes an oasis. Date trees and other plants grow round the pool.

After a sudden rain storm, the desert is covered with flowers. Their seeds lie in the sand until there is enough water for them to grow.

Camels can live for several days without any water. They get very thin and then drink as much as 20 buckets of water at a time.

Hot Wet Places

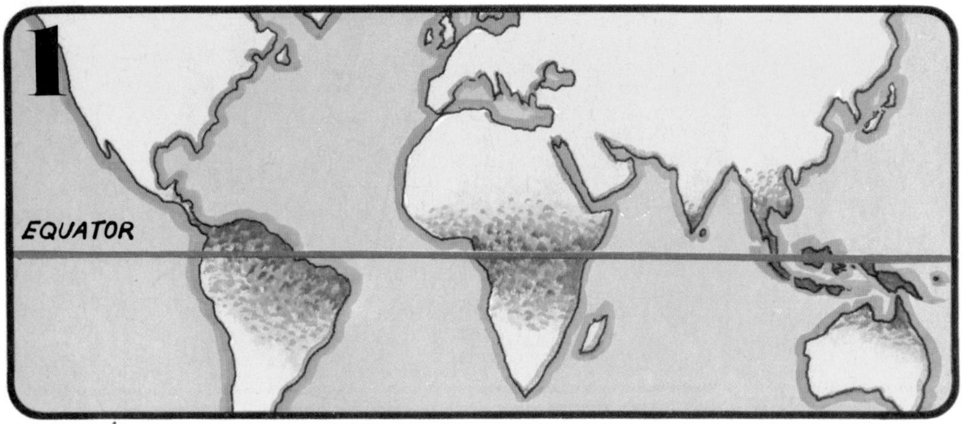

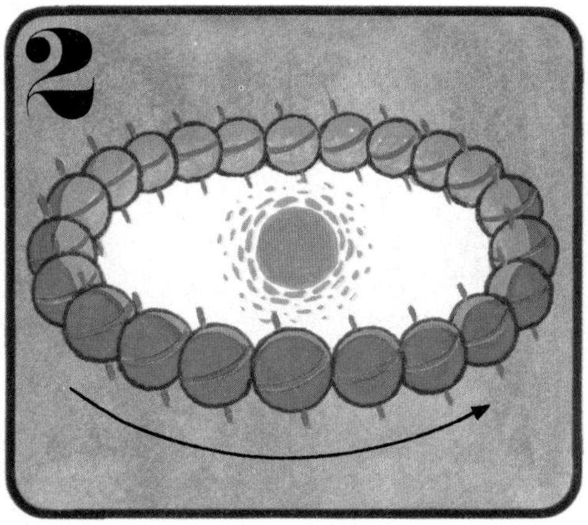

Most of the land round the equator is covered with thick, very green forest, called *rain forest*. It rains heavily nearly every day and there are often thunder storms.

The air is hot and steamy. The plants there like the heat and wetness, and grow very large, with lots of fruit and flowers.

Places near the equator do not have summer and winter. They stay in the Sun's hottest rays all year round, so the wéather never gets cold.

Inside the rain forest it is dark and shady. Some of the trees are higher than a ten-storey office block. They have thick trunks with huge roots to support them.

The trees are like big umbrellas, keeping most of the sunlight out of the forest. A thick tangle of plants fights for any light that seeps through to the forest floor.

Plants with long, rope-like stems hang from the trees. They are called lianas. The stems are strong and are sometimes used for making rope bridges.

The easiest way to travel through rain forest is to follow a river. The trees and lianas grow so thickly along the river banks that you cannot see into the forest.

Rain forest is always green and there are brightly coloured fruits and flowers all year round. The trees do not all lose their leaves at the same time because there is no cold season.

Most of the animals that live in the forest can climb or fly. They need to be able to reach food that grows very high up.

Icy Places

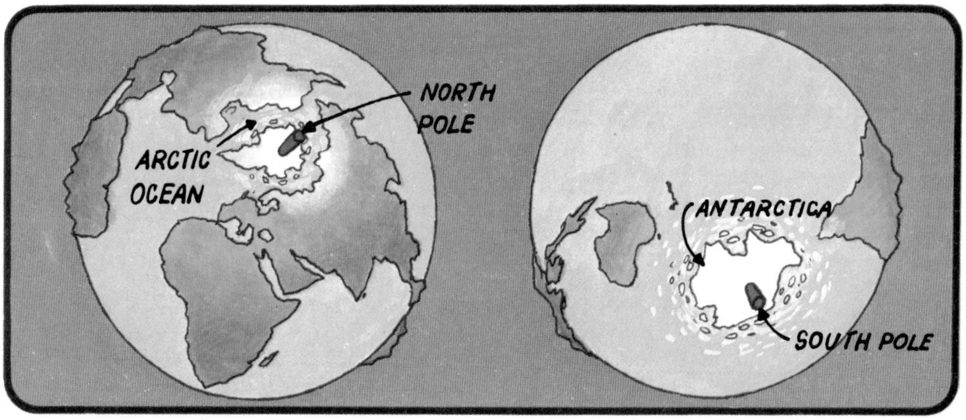

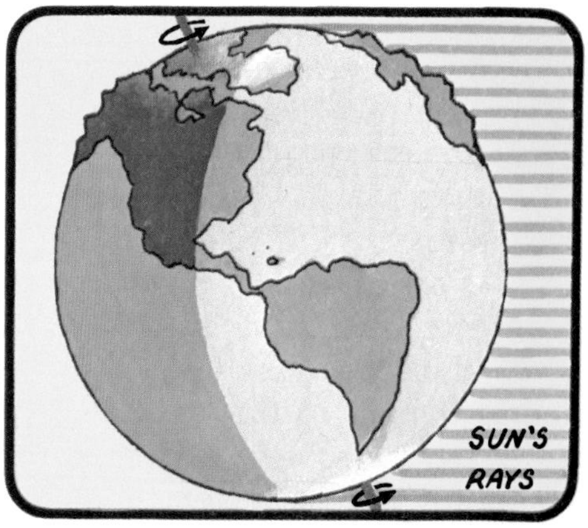

Thick ice covers the North and South Poles all the year. There is no land at the North Pole. An enormous slab of ice floats on the Arctic Ocean.

At the South Pole, the ice covers a big piece of land called Antarctica. Daylight at the Poles lasts for six months at a time. It is dark for the rest of the year.

The Poles do not move in and out of the sunlight when the Earth spins round. This is because the Earth is tilted. One Pole is in daylight, while the other is dark.

At the South Pole

The land at the South Pole was discovered only 150 years ago.

In winter, the sea round Antarctica is frozen. Some of the ice melts in summer. Then, strongly built ships called icebreakers can push their way through to the land.
The only people who live in Antarctica are scientists. They study the rocks and the ice there. The ice is so deep that only the tops of high mountains stick up above it.
Scientists have found coal in the rocks under the snow. Coal is made from trees, so Antarctica must once have been warm enough for trees to grow.
Penguins and other birds live by the sea and catch fish. Further inland, the largest animal is a fly. There are no other animals because there is nothing for them to eat.
Seals and whales live in the sea round Antarctica. They move north when the sea freezes. These animals have a thick layer of fat under their skin which helps to keep them warm.
Antarctica is sometimes called a cold desert because it is so bare and lifeless. A few tiny plants such as mosses grow where there is no ice.

How a Town Grows

Hundreds of years ago most of our towns were small villages. The remains of the villages were buried as new houses and roads were built. Sometimes, people dig up clues which help us to piece together the history of a town.

The first villages were built where people could grow their food. They needed good soil and a spring for water. They looked for a place they could defend from their enemies.

This is the story of how villages grow into towns.

Looking at towns

This is a town we have made up. In many ways it is probably like towns you know. Most towns have houses, shops and offices, factories, roads and bridges. The houses and streets may look different, but can you see how this town is like towns you know?

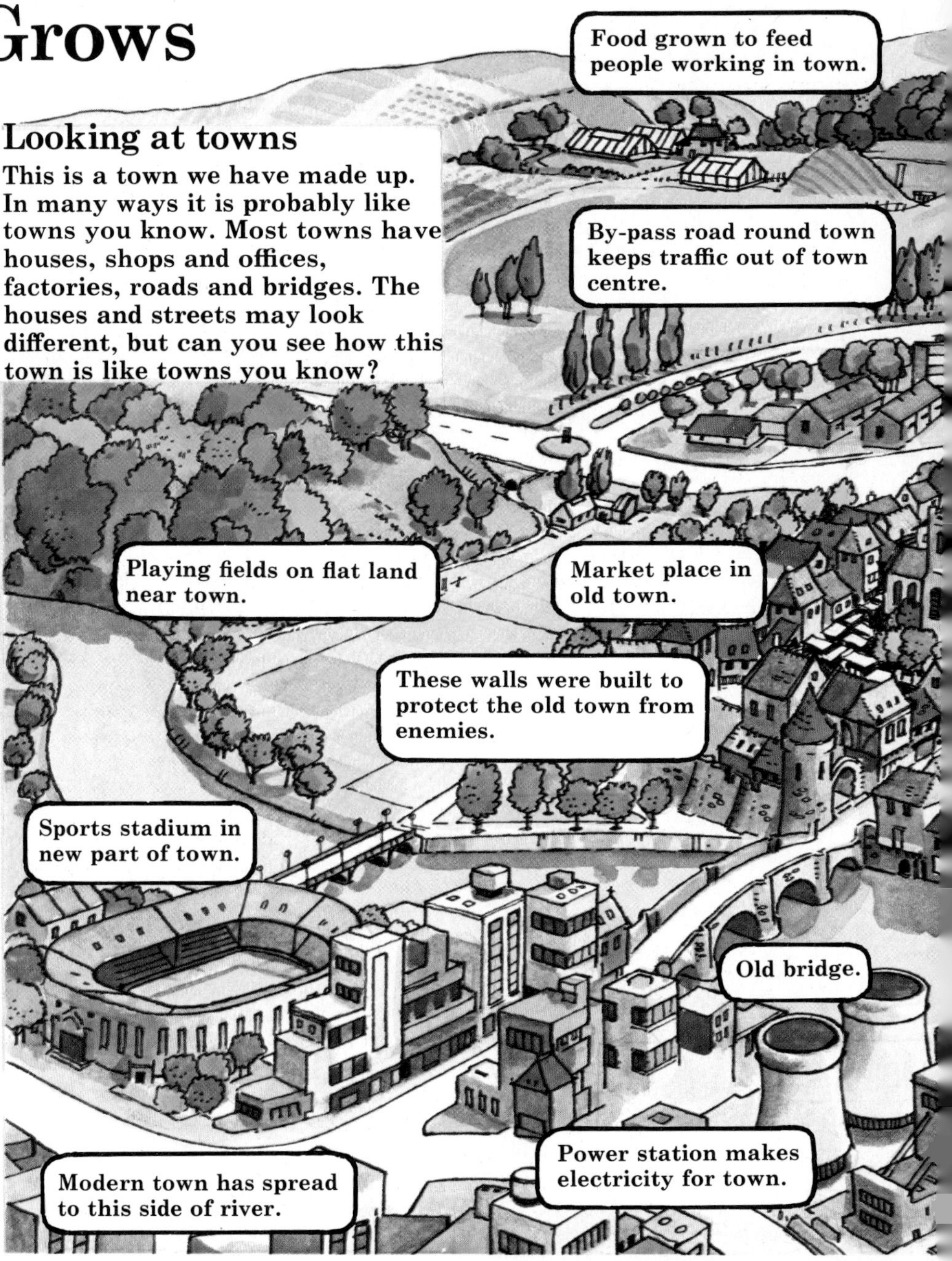
Food grown to feed people working in town.
By-pass road round town keeps traffic out of town centre.
Playing fields on flat land near town.
Market place in old town.
These walls were built to protect the old town from enemies.
Sports stadium in new part of town.
Old bridge.
Modern town has spread to this side of river.
Power station makes electricity for town.

1

The first people on Earth probably did not build houses. They wandered over the countryside, hunting animals and picking berries to eat, and slept in caves.

2

Later, people learnt how to plant seeds and grow food. They tamed wild animals so they did not need to hunt. They settled in one place, built houses and tended the farms.

3

At first people only grew food for themselves. Later, they grew fruit and vegetables to sell. Some villages became market towns where people did their shopping.

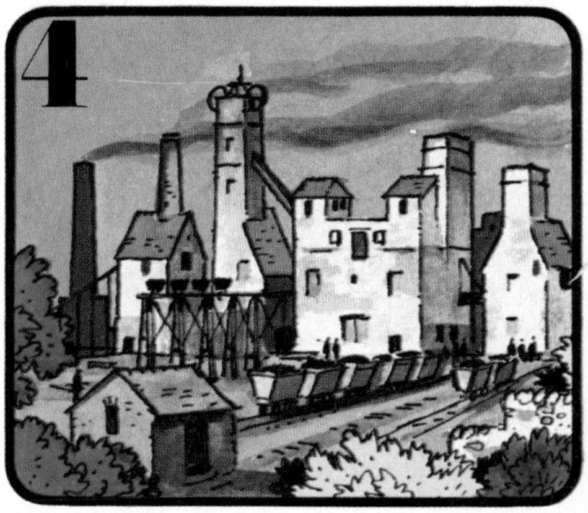
4

About 200 years ago, lots of factories were built near iron and coal mines. Large towns grew up as people moved to work in the new factories.

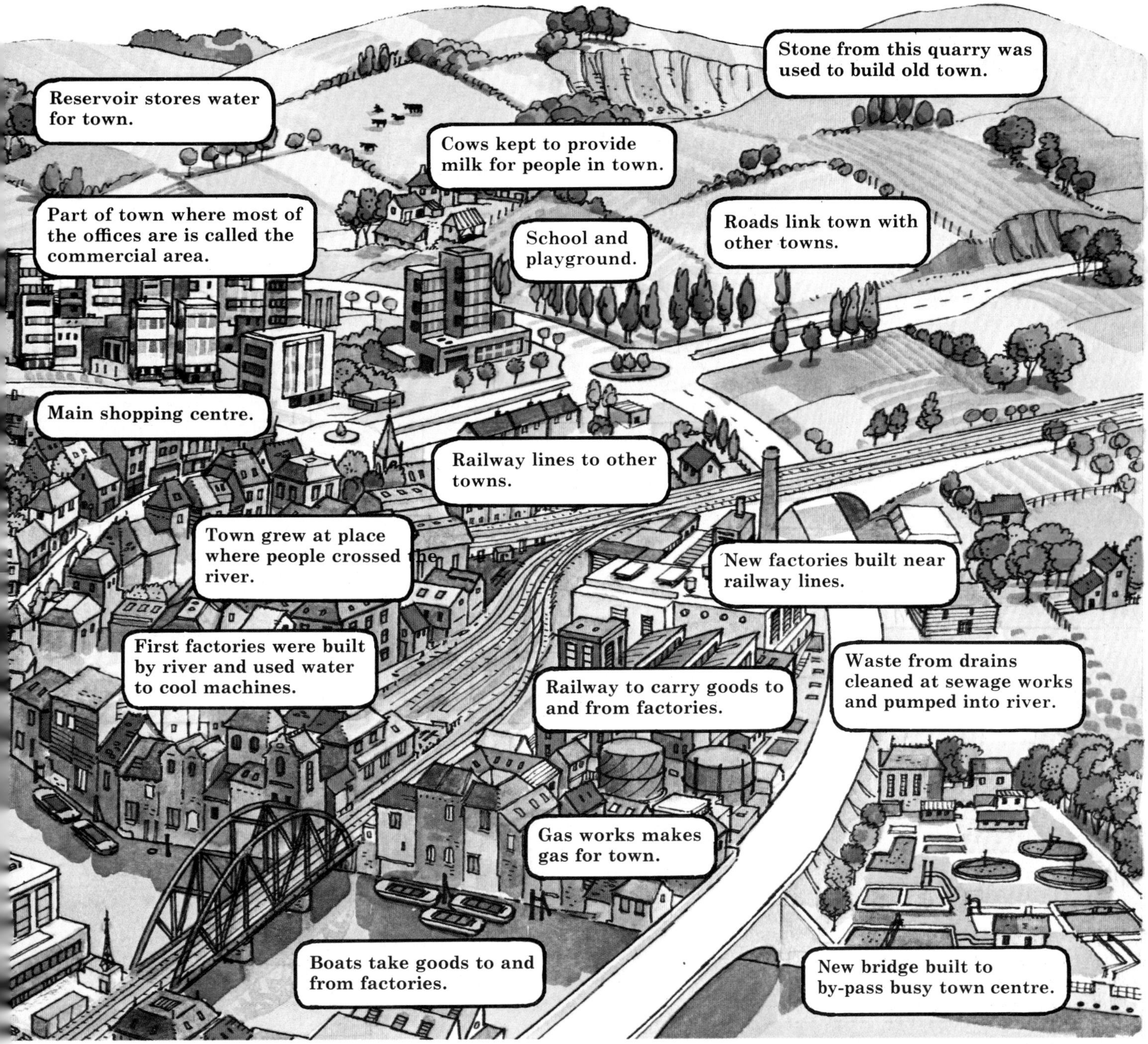

The following labels appear on the illustration:

- Reservoir stores water for town.
- Stone from this quarry was used to build old town.
- Cows kept to provide milk for people in town.
- Part of town where most of the offices are is called the commercial area.
- School and playground.
- Roads link town with other towns.
- Main shopping centre.
- Railway lines to other towns.
- Town grew at place where people crossed the river.
- New factories built near railway lines.
- First factories were built by river and used water to cool machines.
- Railway to carry goods to and from factories.
- Waste from drains cleaned at sewage works and pumped into river.
- Gas works makes gas for town.
- Boats take goods to and from factories.
- New bridge built to by-pass busy town centre.

5 The first settlements by the sea were fishing villages. When people began to travel and sell goods to other countries, some villages grew into huge seaports.

6 Some towns in the mountains or by the sea have become holiday resorts. These towns have lots of hotels, restaurants and shops to serve the holidaymakers.

7 This is a ghost town. The people left because there was no work for them. This happened to many gold-mining towns when all the gold had gone.

Rock Spotter's Guide

There are hundreds of different kinds of rocks, but every rock is either sedimentary, igneous or metamorphic.

You might like to try and identify a piece of rock. These are some of the things to look for in it.

1. Can you see layers?
2. Are there any fossils?
3. Does it feel rough or glassy?
4. Is it made up of tiny grains?
5. Is it a very hard rock?

Here are some of the more common rocks you might find.

Igneous rocks

Rocks made when hot, liquid rock from inside the Earth cools and hardens.

Granite

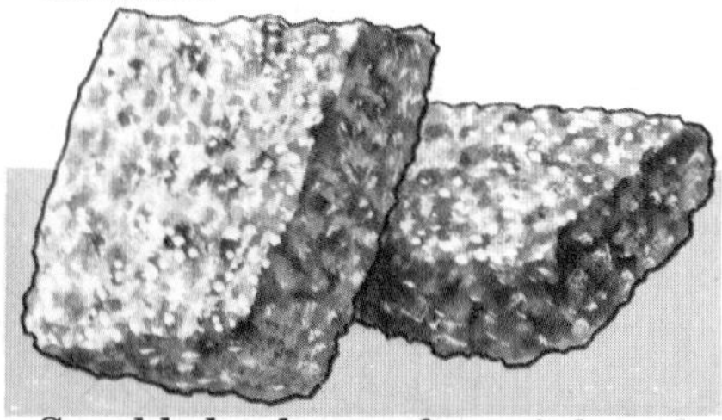

Speckled colour, often pink and grey, or white and grey. Glittery bits in it. Very hard rock.

Basalt

Very hard, black rock. Feels rough and heavy.

Obsidian

Shiny black rock. Feels very smooth and glassy. Often has sharp edges. Also called volcanic glass.

Pumice stone

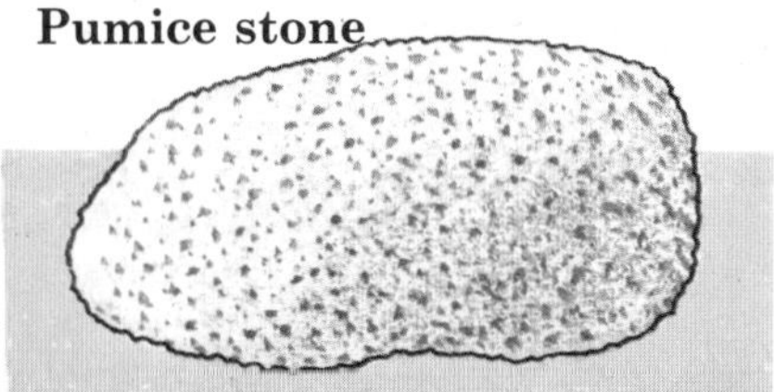

Pale coloured rock with air holes in it. So light that it can float in water.

Sedimentary rocks

Layered rock made from bits of other rocks or shells. Layers do not always show in a small piece, but there may be fossils.

Chalk

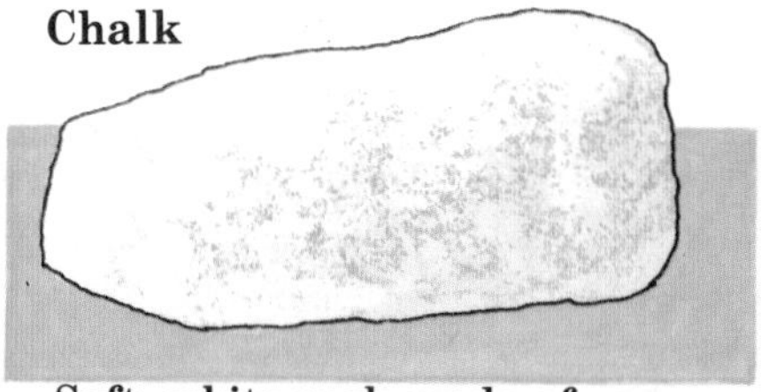

Soft, white rock made of very fine grains. Makes a white mark if you rub it on something hard.

Limestone

Grey, white or yellow rock. Sometimes very hard. You may be able to see fossils and layers.

Sandstone

Rock made from grains of sand. Often you can see layers. Feels rough and sand rubs off it.

Conglomerate

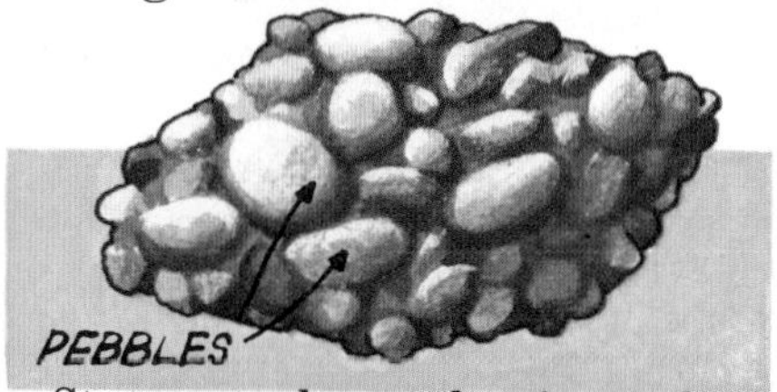

Stones stuck together in sandy rock. The stones are often smooth, rounded pebbles.

Metamorphic rocks

Rocks which have been changed by being heated or squeezed inside the Earth.

Gneiss (pronounced "nice")

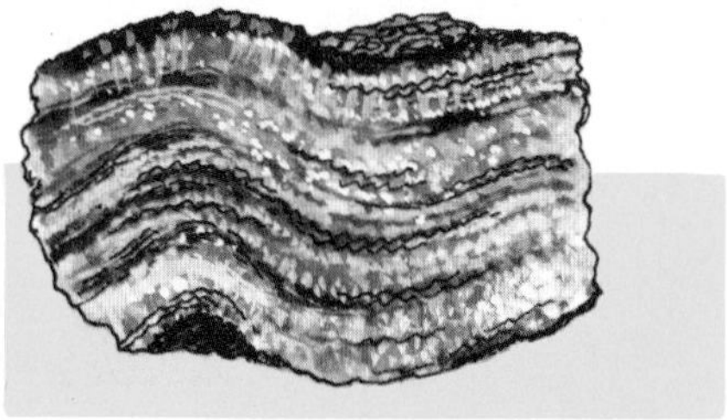

Rock with bands of colour which are often very curvy. Feels rough and glitters.

Schist (pronounced "shist")

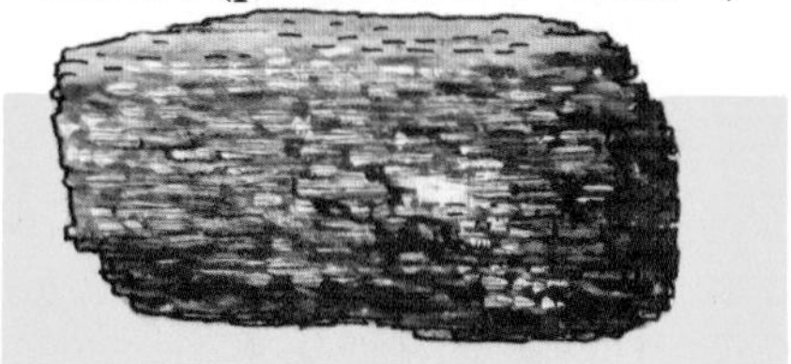

Rock with very thin layers which may be straight or wiggly. Splits along layers. Often glitters.

Slate

Dark-grey rock with layers which easily split apart. Surface of each layer quite smooth.

Marble

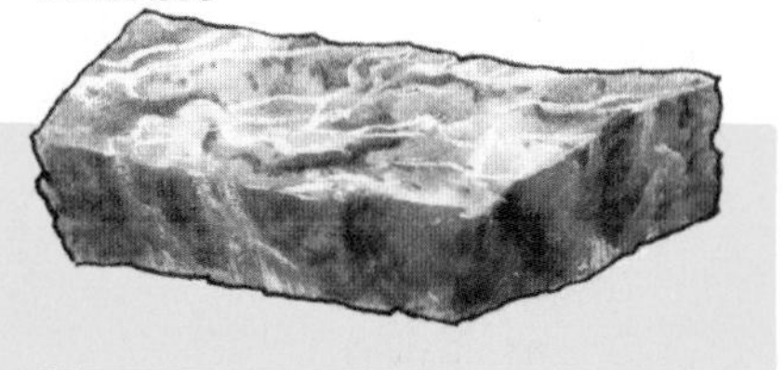

May be pure white or have swirly bands of colour in it. Feels rough and grainy.

Earth Words

Atmosphere
Blanket of air 550 km thick round the Earth.

Axis
Line through the middle of the Earth from north to south.

Core
Centre of the Earth. Probably made of very hot, liquid metal.

Crater (Moon)
Hollows on the Moon's surface.

Crater (Volcano)
Hollow in a volcano where the molten rock comes out.

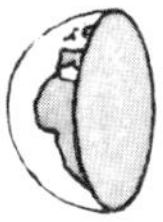

Crust
Earth's shell of solid rock up to 64 km thick.

Delta
Land made from sand, mud and stones dropped by a river when it flows into the sea.

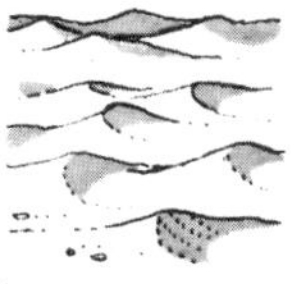

Desert
Land which is so dry that very few plants can grow.

Earthquake
The shuddering and cracking of the Earth caused by rocks moving deep in the Earth.

Equator
Line round the widest part of the Earth.

Fossil
Shape preserved in rock, of an animal or plant which lived long ago.

Galaxy
A group of hundreds of millions of stars.

Geyser
A fountain of hot water which spurts up from under the ground.

Glacier
A mass of ice moving slowly down a mountain.

Hemisphere
Half a sphere. The two halves of the Earth are called the northern hemisphere and the southern hemisphere.

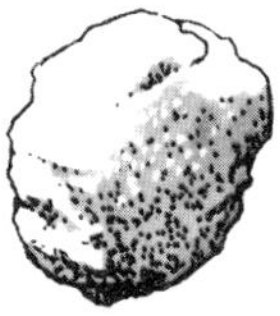

Igneous rock
Rock made when hot, liquid rock from inside the Earth cools and hardens.

Magma
The hot, liquid rock inside the Earth.

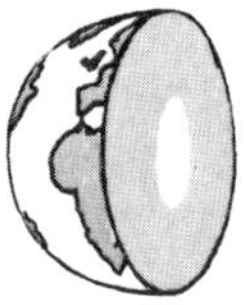

Mantle
The part of the Earth which is made of hot, liquid rock.

Meander
Hairpin bend in a river.

Metamorphic rock
Rock which has been changed by being heated or squeezed inside the Earth.

Moon
A ball of rock in space which goes round a planet.

Oasis
Place in a desert where the water in the ground reaches the surface and plants can grow.

Ox-bow lake
Lake made from the bit of a river left when a river breaks its banks and stops flowing round a bend.

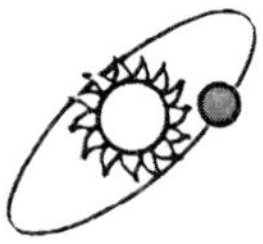

Planet
A ball of rock or gas which goes round a star and does not give out light.

Plate
One piece of the Earth's crust.

Pole
One end of the Earth's axis. The North Pole is at the top and the South Pole is at the bottom.

Satellite
A moon or other object in space which goes round a planet or star.

Sedimentary rock
Rock made from pieces of other rocks or shells.

Snow line
Height above which there is snow all the year on a mountain.

Spur
The part of a hill which sticks across a valley at a bend in a river.

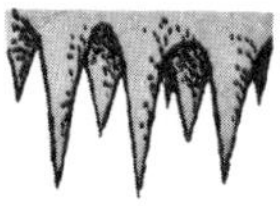

Stalactite
Fingers of rock on the roof of a limestone cave.

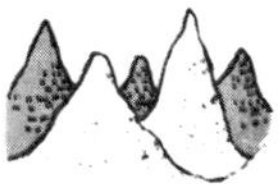

Stalagmite
Columns of rock on the floor of a limestone cave.

Star
A ball of gases in space which gives out heat and light.

Tree line
Height where trees stop growing on a mountain.

Tributary
A river which flows into another river.

Volcano
Place where hot, liquid rock breaks through the Earth's crust.

Index

Numbers written in italics, like this: *8*, show where a word is explained for the first time.